This book should be returned to any branch of the
Lancashire County Library on or before the date shown

20ᵗʰ Aug		HWH

Lancashire County Library,
County Hall Complex,
1st floor Christ Church Precinct,
Preston, PR1 8XJ

Lancashire
County
Council

www.lancashire.gov.uk/libraries

LL1(A)

D0542770

THE
BILLIONAIRE'S
RUTHLESS
AFFAIR

THE BILLIONAIRE'S RUTHLESS AFFAIR

BY

MIRANDA LEE

MILLS & BOON

First published in Great Britain 2016
By Mills & Boon, an imprint of HarperCollins*Publishers*
1 London Bridge Street, London, SE1 9GF

Large Print edition 2016

© 2016 Miranda Lee

ISBN: 978-0-263-26252-0

Printed and bound in Great Britain
by CPI Antony Rowe, Chippenham, Wiltshire

1355341505

CHAPTER ONE

I SHOULD BE HAPPIER, Alex thought as he picked up his mug of coffee and carried it out onto the terrace of his penthouse apartment, shivering slightly when the crisp air hit his face. Not that it would be cold for long, the sun already peeping over the horizon. Winter in Sydney was a picnic compared to winter in London. He *was* glad to be back home. But not all that happy, for some reason.

Alex surveyed the panoramic view of the city skyline, telling himself that a man would have to be a fool not to be happy when he'd finally achieved everything he'd ever vowed to achieve.

At thirty-four, Alex was no fool. He was, in fact, a very successful businessman.

A Rhodes scholar, Alex had first become an entrepreneur back in England over a decade earlier, going into partnership with his two best friends from Oxford in a dilapidated old wine bar, which probably should have been demolished, but which they'd turned into a going concern. As it turned out, one wine bar had eventually become two, then three, then ten, till finally they'd formed a franchise.

Sergio's idea, that.

Alex smiled for the first time that morning. Thinking of Sergio always brought a smile to his face. Jeremy, too. Yet those two were as different as chalk and cheese. Sergio was inclined to take life way too seriously at times, whereas Jeremy... Lord, where did one start with Jeremy? Though some people might describe him as a playboy, Alex knew Jeremy was a decent man at heart, generous and loyal, though with way too much charm and money for his own good. And he'd have even more money now, the recent sale of their wine bar franchise having made them all billionaires.

Alex's smile faded somewhat as he realised that the sale of their franchise had now severed the main connection between the three men. Whilst he didn't doubt they would always remain friends, it would not be the same as when they'd gathered together in London on a regular basis. Sergio had now returned to Milan to take up the reins of his family's ailing manufacturing business, whilst he himself would have no reason to return to England.

Still, that was life, Alex supposed. Nothing stayed the same. Time and tide waited for no man, he knew, a quick glance at his watch showing that it was almost eight.

He was going to be late for work, which was a rarity.

Harry would be wondering where he was. Alex hoped she wasn't upset over the way he'd spoken to her yesterday. Not that she'd seemed offended. Though relatively young, she was without doubt the best, most sensible PA he'd ever had.

Gulping down the rest of his coffee, he hurried back inside, stashed his mug in the dishwasher, snatched up his phone and keys, then headed for the lift. Just as the lift doors opened, his phone rang. A wry smile lit up Alex's face when he saw that it was Jeremy.

Speak of the devil!

'Jeremy…mate…I was just thinking about you.' Alex strode into the lift and pressed the button for the basement car park.

'That's a worry,' Jeremy replied in that deeply masculine voice which always surprised people. 'Haven't you got anything better to do with your life? You should be out there making more millions. Though, perhaps not. You'd only give the lot away.'

Alex grinned. 'You've been drinking, haven't you?' It would be late evening in London.

'You could say that. I'm at a party. An engagement party.'

Alex suppressed a groan at the thought that another one of Jeremy's brothers—perhaps even his mother or father—were on their way to the altar again. You didn't have to look far to understand Jeremy's negative attitude towards love and marriage. Clearly, he didn't trust either to last.

Alex wasn't into love and marriage himself, either, but not for reasons of scepticism and cynicism. He knew full well that true love existed and lasted, if you found the right person. Alex just wasn't interested in finding his soul mate. He had personal reasons for staying a bachelor, the main one being the promise he'd made to his mother on her deathbed.

'God made you extra smart for a purpose, son,'

she'd told him with her last breath. 'Promise me you won't waste your talents. Use them for good. Make a difference.'

Alex had done just that. But being a dedicated philanthropist took a lot of time and energy. He simply didn't have enough left over for a wife and family. Though, if he was strictly honest, Alex liked being a bachelor. Liked living by himself. Liked being free of emotional entanglements.

The lift doors opened at the basement and Alex headed for his nearby SUV at a clip.

'So who's getting hitched this time?' he asked Jeremy. 'Not your mother, I hope.' Jeremy's mother had divorced her third husband last year after she'd discovered he was sleeping with his personal trainer.

'No, thank God. No, this is someone far more surprising.'

'Really?' The mind boggled. 'Look, hold it a sec. Have to get in my car. I'm on my way to work.' Alex jumped in behind the wheel and swiftly connected his phone to Bluetooth. 'Right. All systems go,' he said as he backed out of his spot.

'Do you ever do anything except work?' Jeremy said drily.

'Sure I do. I eat out, work out and have lots of great sex. A bit like you, dear friend.'

'Are you still dating that Lisa chick, the girl you told me about with the grating giggle? Or did you break up with her as you said you were going to as soon as you got back to Sydney?'

'Yeah, she's gone,' Alex said with a scowl on his face. Lisa was still a sore point with him. He'd been going to tell her tactfully this last weekend that it was over between them when she'd actually had the hide to break up with him first, informing him that she'd taken a job on a cruise ship that was setting sail for Asia that very week.

He should have been relieved. Instead, he'd felt decidedly disgruntled. 'I don't want to talk about Lisa,' Alex ground out. 'I want to know which surprising person is getting married.'

'Trust me when I say that you're going to be more than surprised. It's Sergio. *He's* the one getting married.'

Though slightly taken aback, Alex was not exactly shocked. 'What's so surprising about that? He said he was going to find himself a wife when he got back to Italy. It is a bit quick, though.'

Jeremy laughed. 'You don't know the half of it. The wedding's set for just over two weeks' time.'

'Good grief! Why all the hurry? The bride-to-be can't possibly be pregnant. He's only been back in Italy a little over a fortnight.'

'As far as I know, Bella's not pregnant.'

Alex's foot slammed on the brake, bringing an angry hoot of the horn from the car behind him. He was on the car park exit ramp at the time. Gathering himself, he drove on, trying to stay calm and not cause an accident.

'You shouldn't tell me something like that when I'm driving,' he said a lot more calmly than he was feeling. For Bella was *the* Bella, the darling of Broadway and Sergio's one-time stepsister. Sergio had confessed to his friends a couple of years back that he'd always had the hots for her. Naturally, they'd both urged him to move on and forget her.

Clearly, he hadn't taken their advice.

'Trust me, I'm just as shocked as you are,' Jeremy said in droll tones. 'Even worse, I've had to witness Sergio's crazed obsession first-hand.'

'What do you mean?'

'I knew Sergio was staying at his villa on Lake

Como, so I decided to fly over yesterday and surprise him for his birthday.'

'Oh, God, his birthday. I forgot, as usual.'

'You always forget birthdays. Anyway, back to my story. Naturally, I thought Sergio would be alone. He'd said he wanted a holiday before tackling the family business. Apparently, I'd got that wrong. Because when I arrived, he was in Milan, with Bella installed at the villa. She claimed she was suffering from burnout and had tried to rent the villa from Sergio, but he'd invited her to stay as his guest instead.'

Alex's teeth clenched down hard in his jaw. 'So the upshot is she wangled her way back into Sergio's life and then seduced him.'

'That's not how Sergio tells it. He says *he* seduced *her.*'

'That doesn't sound like Sergio.'

'I agree, but apparently he did. And then the poor bastard fell in love with her.'

'Yes, but did she fall in love with him back, or is this a case of like mother like daughter?' Bella's mother was a cold-blooded, ambitious woman who'd married Sergio's widowed father to finance her daughter's singing and dancing career, then divorced him once Bella's career had taken off. 'Does Bella know he's a billionaire now?'

'Don't know. It's been a madhouse here.'

Alex rolled his eyes. 'You must have got some impression of Bella's sincerity. Or lack of it.'

'Well, as unlikely as this will sound coming from an old cynic like me, I think she might be genuinely in love with Sergio.'

'Don't forget she's an actress,' Alex pointed out sharply.

'Now who's being a cynic? Anyway, the wedding's set for the thirty-first of July. I have no doubt that Sergio will be in contact with you shortly. He wants us both to be his best men. I told him we'd be honoured. So when he asks you, try to act thrilled, because there's no way he's going to change his mind about this. The man's crazy about her. All we can do is be there for him to pick up the pieces if and when everything goes belly-up.'

Alex wasn't sure how much help he could be from Australia. But of course he would go to the wedding. He would be proud to stand at Sergio's side as his best man.

'Just book a flight that will get you to Lake Como the day before the wedding. No, make that two days before. I want to take you into Milan and have you fitted with a decent dinner suit. This might prove to be a disastrous marriage, but that's no excuse not to look our very best. We must do Sergio proud on the day. We are, after all, his best men.'

A lump formed in Alex's throat, rendering him speechless for a moment. Fortunately, Jeremy wasn't similarly afflicted.

'Have to go now, Alex. Claudia has just come out onto the terrace looking for me. Now, don't forget to book your flight, and for pity's sake sound thrilled when Sergio calls you. *Ciao*,' he said with a wry laugh. 'When in Rome, you know.' And he hung up.

Alex groaned at the thought of having to sound thrilled when Sergio contacted him. But he would do it for Sergio's sake. Fate wasn't being kind to him, letting him fall for a woman like Bella. Their getting married was a disaster waiting to happen.

Such thinking reinforced Alex's own decision never to get tangled up in the whole 'love and

marriage' thing. Loving and losing someone—
either through death or divorce—was never going
to be on his agenda. No way would he risk ending up like his father, or becoming the victim of
some clever gold-digger. That was why he always
dated girls who never had a hope of ensnaring
his heart. Girls who just wanted to have fun.

Alex quickly realised there would be no time
for fun during the next two weeks. His nose
would be pressed to the grindstone every single
day. At least it would be when he finally got to
the damned office. Poor Harry. She was probably
close to sending out a search party!

Harriet didn't mind at all that her boss was running late that morning. When she'd arrived at
the office shortly before eight, she'd been dread-
ing having to tell him her news, news which she
should have told him when he'd first come back
from London. But at the time her emotions had
been too raw. She would have wept in front of
him. She knew she would. And she didn't want
to do that. Alex would have been embarrassed.
And so would she.

So she'd let the days tick away without confessing that her engagement to Dwayne was no more, her anxiety increasing as each day passed. She'd rather hoped her boss might notice that she wasn't wearing her engagement ring, but he hadn't. Alex didn't notice personal details like that. He was a man with tunnel vision most of the time. When at work, he worked.

It did irk Harriet slightly that no one else at Ark Properties had noticed, either. But that was her fault. Whilst she was friendly with everyone who worked there, she didn't socialise with the rest of the staff. She never went with them for drinks on a Friday night. Harriet had her own group of girlfriends she had drinks with, Emily of course being the main one. Then of course, up till recently, she'd had Dwayne.

Naturally, things would be different from now on, with no Dwayne to complain if she didn't hurry home after work. It worried Harriet, however, that her suddenly single status would change the wonderful working relationship she'd always had with Alex. He was a great boss. She liked him a lot and felt sure that he liked her back. Yet when she'd walked into his office to be interviewed for the job last year, Harriet had gained the immediate impression that she was a non-starter. Alex had looked her up and down with sceptical eyes. With hindsight, maybe he'd been worried that she might make a play for him. He was, after all, one of Sydney's most eligible bachelors.

Whatever; as soon as he'd discovered she was engaged, his attitude had changed. Though he'd still put her through the mill during the interview. She must have pleased him with her answers, because he'd hired her on the spot.

Of course, her résumé *had* been second to none—provided you overlooked her poor pass in her Higher School Certificate. Which Alex had, once she'd explained that her dad—who was a miner—had lost his job during her high school years and that the family finances had been so tight that she'd taken not one but *three* part-time positions to help make ends meet, her studies suffering as a result. A little white lie, that. But not one she felt guilty about. The boss of Ark Properties didn't need to know the ins and outs of her past life. Alex had seemed suitably impressed by her work ethic, plus her career in real estate. He didn't care that she'd never actually been a PA before. He wanted someone who could take over the office whenever he was away, which up till recently had been quite often. He had business ties in England which she wasn't privy to; Alex could be secretive at times.

But those business ties had apparently been wound up and he was back in Sydney permanently. Harriet might have felt pleased if she hadn't been in a state of apprehension at the time. That apprehension had now reached such a level that it was interfering with her sleep. So Harriet had resolved last night to bite the bullet and tell Alex the truth this morning. Which would have happened already if he'd been here when she'd arrived, she thought with a flash of irritation. All of a sudden, his being late didn't seem quite so desirable, the delay in confessing twisting her stomach into more knots.

Sighing at the sight of Alex's empty office, she headed straight for the staff room, where she filled the kettle in readiness for the mug of black coffee Alex always wanted first thing on arriving. He'd probably send her out for a bagel, too. That man was a bagel addict! Maybe she'd leave off telling him her news till he'd downed his coffee and bagel. Alex wasn't at his best till he'd eaten. The kettle on, she opened the over-head cupboard and took down one of the small tins of quite expensive cat food she kept there. The snapping sound of the ring pull had a rather large moggy dashing into the room, purring his welcome as he wound his way around Harriet's ankles.

'Hungry, Romany?' Harriet said, quickly scrap-ing the food out onto a saucer and putting it down on the floor. The cat pounced, gobbling up the food like he was starving.

'You spoil that cat.'

Harriet whirled at the sound of Alex's voice, surprised that she hadn't heard him come in. He looked impossibly handsome as usual, dressed in a dark blue business suit which deepened the blue of his eyes and contrasted nicely with the fair hair. His shirt was a dazzling white, his tie a stylish blue-and-silver stripe.

'You ought to talk,' Harriet said, thinking of all her boss had done for Romany. 'Might I remind you that *you* were the one who insisted on buy-ing all the top-of-the-line cat accessories.'

'Had to do something to stop my PA from crying her eyes out.'

'I wasn't doing any such thing.'

'You were close to,' he reminded her.

I suppose I was, she thought as she picked up the plate, washed it thoroughly and put it away, not wanting any of the staff to start complaining about the smell of fishy cat food. Not that they would. They all loved Romany. Unlike Dwayne. He hadn't loved Romany at all; had complained like mad when Harriet had brought the poor starving animal home a couple of months ago after she'd found him cowering and crying under her car one Saturday night. He'd insisted she take it to the RSPCA the very next day, which she had, hopeful that they would find him a good home.

Impossible, they'd said. No one would want a seriously old cat like Romany. Unable to bear leaving him there to be put down, in desperation she'd taken him to work on the Monday, where she'd asked if anyone would give him a home. When no one had put their hand up, Alex had said he could be the office cat. Always a man of action, he'd immediately had a cat flap installed in the store room, then had taken Harriet out to buy whatever was necessary to keep the cat happy and clean. The cleaners had been informed of Romany's presence so that precautions could be taken for him not to escape.

Harriet recalled feeling overwhelmed by Alex's generosity and kindness at the time whilst seething with resentment over Dwayne's meanness. As she bent and scooped the cat up in her arms, she realised that the incident with Romany had been the beginning of the end of their relationship. Being an animal lover was, after all, one of her checklist points. After that, she'd begun to look at Dwayne with different eyes. The rose-coloured glasses that came with falling in love had definitely come off. His constant refusal to give any money to charity was a sore point. So was his not doing his share of housework around the flat. When she'd complained to Emily about this, she'd just laughed, saying Harry expected way too much from men.

'They expect their women to look after *them*,' her best friend had told her. 'It's in their DNA.

They're the protectors and providers, whilst their women are the homemakers and nurturers.'

Harriet hadn't agreed with Emily, hoping the world had moved on from expecting women to be happy with such narrow roles in life. No way was she going to settle for less than what she wanted in life, which was an interesting career, as well as a husband who ticked all of the boxes on her Mister Right checklist. Dwayne had certainly ticked the first three, but had begun seriously falling down on the rest. His suggestion a month ago that she buy her wedding dress second-hand on the Internet had been the last straw!

'So has the kettle boiled?' Alex asked, interrupting Harriet's none-too-happy thoughts.

'Should have,' she said.

Dropping the cat gently on the tiled floor, she set about getting two mugs down from the overhead cupboard. 'It's not like you to be late,' she added, doing her best to ignore the instant churning in her stomach. Maybe she wouldn't tell him today after all...

'I slept in,' he replied. 'Then traffic was bad. I'm going to need a bagel with my coffee.'

'Fine. Oh, and, Alex...' she said before he had

the opportunity to walk away and before she could procrastinate further. 'When you have a minute, I…um…I need to talk to you about something.'

He sighed a rather weary-sounding sigh. 'Look, Harry, if you're going to complain about the way I spoke to you yesterday, then don't bother. I'm sorry. All right? I was in a bad mood and I took it out on you, which I realise was unforgiveable, but I'm only human. If you must know, I broke up with Lisa at the weekend.'

'Oh,' she said, not really surprised. Of the three girls Alex had dated during the time she'd worked for him, Lisa had been the most annoying with that silly laugh of hers, not to mention the way she would drop into the office unannounced. Alex hadn't liked that, and neither had Harriet. 'I'm sorry,' she added a little belatedly.

'I'm not. Not really.' Alex stared at her hard for a long moment. 'You're not going to quit, are you?'

Her shocked expression must have soothed him, for his eyes immediately softened. But it underlined to Harriet that Alex was not a man who responded well to being crossed or thwarted. She'd always known he was a tough businessman, but she'd never seen him seriously angry. It wasn't in his nature to be mean, but she suspected he had a temper, like most men.

'No, nothing like that,' she said quickly.

'Then out with it, Harriet. I don't like to wait for bad news.'

'It's not bad news,' she said, startled by his calling her Harriet like that. She'd always liked the way he called her Harry. There was a subtle intimacy about it which made her feel like his friend as well as his assistant. Obviously, she'd been deluding herself in that regard.

'Well, not bad news for you,' she went on sharply, doing her best to control a whole range of emotions which began bombarding her. The sudden lump in her throat alarmed her.

'The thing is, Alex, I…I've broken off my engagement to Dwayne.'

His expression carried a measure of shock, quickly followed by one of genuine sympathy.

When tears pricked at her eyelids, panic was only a heartbeat away.

'I'm very sorry to hear that, Harry,' he said gently. 'Very sorry indeed.'

His calling her Harry like that completed her undoing, bringing a wave of emotion which shattered her pretend composure and sent a torrent of tears into her eyes.

CHAPTER TWO

ALEX'S SHOCK AT Harriet's news was eclipsed by her bursting into tears. For not once during the months she'd worked for him had she ever cried. Or come close to it, except perhaps over the cat. She was the epitome of common sense and composure, pragmatic and practical under pressure at all times. Even when he snapped at her—as he had yesterday—she just ignored him and went on with her job. Which he admired.

He didn't care for women who cried at the drop of a hat or used tears as a weapon. He'd been brought up by a woman who'd been very stalwart by nature, a legacy perhaps of being born poor in war-torn Hungary, she and Alex's father having migrated to Australia when they'd been just newlyweds. They'd hoped to make a better life down under. Unfortunately, that hadn't happened. But his mother had never complained, or cried.

'Crying doesn't get you anywhere,' his mother had told her three children often enough.

She had cried, however, when she'd found out she was dying of cervical cancer, a condition which could have been cured if she'd been diagnosed early enough.

Don't think about that, Alex. Attend to the here and now. Which is your usually calm PA sobbing her broken heart out.

After standing in the doorway for far too long, wondering how he'd forgotten that Harry was a woman with a woman's more sensitive emotions, Alex launched himself across the room and gathered her into his arms.

'There, there,' he said soothingly as he stroked her soft brown hair.

If anything she sobbed even harder, her shoulders shaking as her hands curled into fists and pressed against his chest. Romany meowed plaintively at his feet, obviously sensing distress in the air.

'Stop crying now,' he advised gently. 'You're upsetting the cat.'

She didn't stop crying and Romany ran off, the insensitive deserter. Alex wished he could do likewise. He didn't feel entirely comfortable holding Harry like this. He was never comfortable with excess emotion. Neither was he a touchy-feely kind of guy. He touched a woman only when he was about to make love to her.

'Oh! S-sorry.'

Alex's head swivelled round at the sound of Audrey's startled apology. Audrey was forty, divorced and a cynic and the expression on his receptionist's face suggested she'd instantly jumped to the conclusion that something of an intimate nature was going on between her boss and his PA. Alex knew he had to nip that idea in the bud before nasty rumours started flying around the office.

'Harriet is upset,' he said rather brusquely. 'She's broken off her engagement to Dwayne.'

Audrey's finely plucked eyebrows formed an even greater arch. 'Really? What did he do?'

Alex rolled his eyes at the woman's lack of compassion. All she seemed interested in were the grisly details. Though, now that he thought about it, Alex was curious about the circumstances as well. He could not imagine Dwayne being unfaithful. He wasn't that kind of guy. Not that he knew him well. He'd met him only twice.

Alex had actually been surprised by Harriet's choice of fiancé. She was a very attractive girl—and smart as a whip—whereas Dwayne was just, well, ordinary, both in looks and intelligence. Alex had found him quite boring to talk to. He would have expected more interesting conversation from a high school history teacher, but Dwayne had come over as being interested in only his pay cheque and his holidays.

'More time to play golf,' he'd said rather avidly.

Perhaps that was what had gone wrong. Maybe he'd been spending too much time on the golf course and not enough time making love to his fiancée. Alex knew that if he was engaged to Harriet, he would spend quite a lot of time making love to her. Having her in his arms reminded him what a good figure she had.

When such thinking sparked a prickling in his groin, Alex decided to bring a swift end to his hugging Harriet so closely. Stepping back from the embrace, he leaned over to snatch a handful of tissues from the box that was kept on the counter and held them out towards her still-clenched hands.

'Dry your eyes,' he ordered.

She did as she was told, blowing her nose quite noisily.

'Now, I'm taking Harriet out for coffee. And we won't be back for a while,' he relayed to Audrey. 'Let the others know the situation when they come in, will you?'

'Will do,' Audrey replied.

'I...I'd like to fix my face before I go out anywhere,' Harriet requested.

'Fair enough,' Alex said. 'I'll meet you at the lifts in five minutes.'

Grabbing her handbag, Harriet dashed out of the office and along the corridor to the ladies' room, which thankfully was empty. She groaned when the vanity mirror showed flushed cheeks and red-rimmed eyes. Sighing, she splashed them with cold water, glad that she didn't wear eye make-up during the day. Otherwise she might have ended up looking like a raccoon.

Grabbing some paper towels, she dabbed her face dry, after which she swiftly replenished her red lipstick before running a brush through her shoulder-length brown hair. When it fell into its usual sleek curtain without a strand out of place, she conceded that her monthly appointment with one of Sydney's top stylists was worth every cent. It saved her heaps of time every morning and in moments like this. Because, when Alex said he'd meet her in five minutes, he meant five minutes. Patience was not one of her boss's virtues. Kindness was, however. And compassion. He'd shown both with Romany and now with her.

She should have known he'd be nice to her.

Not that she'd expected him to hug her like that. That had been a surprise. So had her bursting into tears in the first place. It wasn't like her to be so emotional. But she supposed it wasn't every day that your dreams for the future were shattered. Maybe if she'd cried buckets during the days after the split with Dwayne, she wouldn't have broken down just now. She hadn't even told Emily, knowing perhaps her friend's critical reaction. She'd just bottled up her feelings, then stupidly started worrying that telling Alex her news would jeopardise her job. As if he would be so cruel as to sack her because she was suddenly single. The very idea was ludicrous!

With a final swift glance at her reflection in the mirror, Harriet hurried from the ladies' room and strode quickly along the grey carpeted corridor which would bring her to the lift well. Alex was already there, his expression shuttered as he looked her up and down, probably searching for signs that she had herself under control. No way would he want her weeping by his side in public. She gave him a small, reassuring smile, but he didn't smile back, his gaze still probing.

'Better now?' he said.

'Much. You don't have to do this, you know,' she added, despite actually wanting to go and have coffee with him. 'We could just go back into the office and have coffee there.'

'Absolutely not. Audrey and the others can hold the fort.'

The lift doors opened and several office workers piled out, Ark Properties not being the only business with rooms on that particular floor, though theirs were the pick, with Alex's office having a wonderful view of the Harbour Bridge and the Opera House. 'Nothing like a good view of Sydney's spectacular icons to help sell property in Australia,' he'd told her on the day he'd hired her.

Harriet agreed wholeheartedly.

'So when did all this happen?' Alex asked her as he waved her into the now empty lift.

'The weekend you flew home from London,' she told him.

He threw a sharp glance over his shoulder as he pressed the ground-floor button.

'Why didn't you tell me straight away?' he went on before she could think of a suitable answer. 'Did you want to give yourself the opportunity to change your mind? Or for Dwayne to change it for you?'

'No. No, once I made up my mind, I knew I wouldn't change it. Dwayne hasn't tried to change my mind, either. After our last argument, he knew it was over between us.'

'That must have been some argument.'

'It was.' A rueful smile teased the corners of her mouth. What would Alex say, she wondered, if he knew he'd been the subject of most of that last argument?

His eyes narrowed on her. 'Want to tell me about it?'

She looked up into his gorgeous blue eyes, then shook her head. 'I don't think that would be a good idea.'

'Well, I do,' he stated firmly just as the lift doors opened on the ground floor. Taking her arm, he steered her across the spacious lobby and through the revolving glass doors which led out onto the chilly city street.

'So which café do you prefer?' he asked, nodding towards each of the two casual eating establishments that flanked the entrance to their building. It occurred to Harriet that Alex had never actually taken her for coffee before. She'd lunched with him a few times—always with clients—but only at the kind of five-star restaurants which catered for businessmen of his status.

'That one has better bagels,' she said, pointing to the café on their left.

'That one it is, then.'

He found them an empty table at one of the windows which overlooked the street, seeing her settled before heading for the counter. Harriet found it odd watching him queue up to order food, thinking he wouldn't have done that too often. But then she recalled that he hadn't always been rich and successful.

When she'd secured a second and personal interview for this job, she'd looked him up on the Internet, unable to find out all that much information, the best being an article written about him for a men's magazine a couple of years back. Harriet had been surprised to discover that he'd come from a down-at-heel migrant family, living in government housing in the outer western suburbs of Sydney. His near-genius IQ had given him access to special schools for gifted children, followed by various financial grants to help him through university, culminating in his being awarded a Rhodes Scholarship.

The magazine article she'd read had outlined his rise to success in Sydney, first as a realtor based mainly in the western suburbs, then as a property developer with his head office in the heart of Sydney's CBD. The article made no mention of any business interests in England, or his personal life, except to say that he was one of Sydney's most eligible bachelors. There'd been no mention of his family or friends.

Harriet rolled her eyes at what happened when Alex reached the front of the queue. The very pretty young brunette behind the counter beamed at him as she took his order, her eyes and manner very flirtatious. Harriet found herself decidedly irritated, hating the thought that Alex might have already found a replacement for that silly Lisa. The sudden thought that she might be jealous seemed ludicrous. Jealous of whom? And of what? And, more to the point, *why*?

Harriet frowned, wondering and worrying that Alex's hugging her earlier might have unlocked feelings which she'd always had for him and which she'd successfully hidden, even from herself. Harriet couldn't deny that she'd liked the feel of his big, strong arms around her; she liked his bringing her here for coffee as well.

Whatever, when Alex turned away from the counter and started heading towards her, Harriet found herself looking at him with new eyes, the same new eyes which had examined Dwayne with brutal honesty and had found him sadly lacking.

The word 'lacking' would never apply to the boss of Ark Properties. He had everything that any woman would want. In a boyfriend, that was, but not in a prospective husband.

So lock this unwanted attraction of yours away again, Harriet, and look elsewhere for your life partner. Because it's never going to be Alex Kotana!

Perversely, however, as soon as he sat back down at their table, she opened her silly, jealous mouth and said waspishly, 'I suppose that happens to you all the time.'

'What?' he said, sounding perplexed.

Whilst kicking herself, Harriet quickly found a wry little smile and a more casual tone. 'The brunette behind the counter didn't half make it clear that you could have put her on your order, if you'd been so inclined.'

Alex smiled. 'She did, didn't she? Unfortunately, she's not my type.'

'You don't like brunettes?' Now that she thought about it, his last two girlfriends had been blondes. She'd never met the first one, who'd come and gone within a month of her becoming Alex's PA, so she didn't know if she was a blonde or not.

His eyes held hers for a rather long moment, making Harriet feel decidedly uncomfortable.

She hoped her momentary jab of jealousy hadn't been obvious earlier. If it had, then she might not be lasting long in her job. It was a depressing thought. Her job meant the world to her. It was interesting and challenging and very well paid. Now that she didn't have Dwayne in her life, she needed her job more than ever.

'Sorry,' she said swiftly. 'I shouldn't be asking you personal questions like that. It's none of my business.'

Alex shrugged his powerful shoulders. 'No sweat. I'm about to ask you a personal question or two.'

'Oh?'

'Come now, Harry, you don't expect me not to be curious over why you broke up with Dwayne. That's why I brought you down here away from the prying eyes and ears in the office. To worm out all the grisly details. You must know that.'

Harriet sighed. 'There are no grisly details.' Just mundane ones.

'So you didn't discover he was a secret drunk, or a drug addict?'

'*No!*'

'You didn't come home and find him in bed with your best friend?'

'Lord no,' she said and laughed.

'Then what on earth did the man do?'

Harriet knew it was going to be difficult to explain without her seeming like some kind of nutcase. But she could see she would have to try. When Alex wanted to know something, he was like a dog with a bone.

'He just didn't measure up as husband material.'

'Ah,' Alex said, as though understanding perfectly what she was talking about. 'I rather suspected that his golf playing might have become a problem.'

Harriet just stared at him. 'I had no problem with Dwayne playing golf,' she replied, feeling somewhat confused. 'Though it didn't go down well when he bought a very expensive set of clubs the same day he suggested I buy my wedding dress on the Internet.'

Alex's brows lifted. 'He wanted you to buy a second-hand wedding dress?'

'Yes,' she admitted tartly.

'Ah,' he said in that knowing way again, Harriet

gratified that her boss understood that Dwayne's penny-pinching suggestion might have been a deal breaker.

'My father was a mean man with money,' she found herself elaborating. 'I vowed when I was just a teenager that I would never marry a scrooge.'

'I fully agree with you. But didn't you know Dwayne was tight with money when you first started dating him?'

'He wasn't like that then. He used to spend money on me like water. Took me to the best restaurants, the best concerts, the best of everything.'

'Yes, well, a man like Dwayne would have had to pull out all stops to impress a girl like you. And he succeeded, didn't he? You fell for him and agreed to marry him. But once he had his ring on your finger, he dropped the ball. Am I right?'

'Very right,' Harriet agreed, then frowned. 'What do you mean by "a girl like me"?'

Alex smiled a crooked smile. 'It must have been very upsetting to find out that your Prince Charming was nothing but a frog. And a stingy frog at that. What I meant was that you were always a cut above Dwayne, not only in looks but in intelligence and personality. He must have known on first meeting you that he would have to lift his game in every department if he wanted to win the heart of the beautiful Harriet Mc-Kenna. But the fool couldn't keep it up, which is what happens when you play out of your league.'

Harriet flushed wildly at his compliments, not sure whether to believe him or not. Alex could be inclined to flattery on occasions. Not with her, but with clients. Though he had said she looked gorgeous the night they'd all attended that fund-raising dinner back in March. She'd been wearing a new red cocktail dress which had looked well on her with her dark hair and eyes.

'So what was the final straw?' Alex went on. 'The wedding dress business? Or something else?'

'The wedding dress suggestion certainly brought things to a head. But I'd been unhappy for some time. And worried. It was obvious Dwayne wasn't the man I thought he was. He certainly wasn't acting like the man I fell in love with. He'd become lazy around the house. And with me.'

'You mean your sex life had suffered.'

Harriet laughed and blushed slightly. 'What sex life?'

'The man was a fool,' Alex said sharply. 'What did he honestly expect would happen if he started neglecting you in bed?'

'I have no idea,' Harriet said with a sigh, thinking to herself that she couldn't imagine Alex neglecting any of his girlfriends in bed. That man had testosterone oozing out of every pore of his gorgeous male body. 'He obviously didn't expect me to break off our engagement. He couldn't believe it at first. When I tried to explain the reasons why I'd fallen out of love with him, he went into a rage, accusing me of all sorts of crazy things.'

'Like what?'

Harriet could see Alex was determined to hear the truth behind the break-up.

'Like I no longer loved him because I'd fallen in love with you...

'As if I'd be stupid enough to do something like that,' she raced on before Alex had a chance to jump to any potentially dangerous conclusions.

CHAPTER THREE

THE ARRIVAL OF the brunette with his order of coffee and bagels could not have come at a better time, giving Alex the opportunity to hide his peeved reaction to Harriet's somewhat scoffing reply to Dwayne's accusation. A perverse reaction, in a way, considering he didn't want any woman falling in love with him. But it wasn't very flattering for Harry to tell him that her falling for him would be *stupid*!

His throwing the waitress one of his super-charming smiles was more the result of a bruised ego than his desire to capture the girl's interest. He'd been right when he'd said she wasn't his type. She'd been way too eager to please. As much as Alex liked to date pretty young things—and the brunette was just that—he preferred independent, spirited girls who didn't gush or grovel, and who didn't have a single gold-digging bone in their bodies. Alex had known immediately that the brunette was not of that ilk.

'Is there anything else you'd like, sir?' the brunette asked after carefully placing the coffee and bagel on the table, her attention all on him, not having cast a single glance in Harriet's direction.

'No, thanks,' he said and resisted the impulse to give her a tip. Harriet was already looking seriously irritated.

As the waitress departed, Harriet sent him a droll look.

'Yes, I know,' he said drily. 'It does happen to me all the time. But she's still not my type.'

'Then perhaps you shouldn't have flirted with her.'

Alex clenched his teeth hard in his jaw whilst he struggled to control his temper. 'And perhaps *you* should tell me why you find me so unlovable,' he retorted, still smarting over her earlier remark.

She blinked at his sharpness before dropping her eyes, taking a few seconds to pour the sugar into her coffee and looking up at him again. 'I never said you were unlovable, Alex. I said I would not be stupid enough to fall in love with you. That's an entirely different concept.'

Alex's bruised ego was not to be so easily mollified. 'Would you care to explain that last statement further? Why would it be so stupid for you to fall in love with me?'

'Aside from the fact that I'm your PA, you mean?' she threw at him.

He had to concede that that was an excellent reason. It was never a good idea to mix business and pleasure, something which he was in danger of forgetting.

'Point taken,' he said. 'Is that the only reason, then?'

She gave him a long, searching look that he found decidedly irritating. This was a Harriet he wasn't used to. Up till today she'd been the perfect PA, never complaining or criticising, calmly obeying his every wish and command. She'd never before looked at him in such an assessing and possibly judgmental fashion. He didn't like it. He didn't like it one bit.

Frankly, he preferred the Harriet who'd wept in his arms.

'You're not eating your bagel,' she said as she

coolly stirred her flat white. 'And your coffee will get cold. You know how you hate lukewarm coffee.'

'I also hate not having my questions answered,' he ground out, sweeping up his mug of black coffee and glaring at her over the rim.

Harriet knew she had annoyed him; knew he'd taken her statement as a personal criticism. It had been seriously foolish of her to tell him about Dwayne's accusation. But it was too late now. Somehow she had to explain her remark without offending Alex further.

Make light of it, girl. Turn it round so that it's your failing and not his. And don't, for pity's sake, repeat the word 'stupid' in context with falling in love with him. No wonder he took umbrage!

'The thing is,' she said in a lighter, less emotional voice, 'I realised a few years back that if I wanted to get married and have children…which I did; which I still do, actually…that I had to stop dating a certain type of man. I—'

'And what type is that?' Alex interrupted before she could go on.

'Oh, you know. *Your* type.'

'*My* type?'

Oh, dear, she'd done it again. She'd opened her big mouth and put her foot in it. 'Well, not exactly your type, Alex,' she said with a 'butter wouldn't melt in her mouth' smile. 'You are rather unique. As you are aware, I've worked in real estate ever since I came to Sydney when I was twenty. Girls usually date men they meet at work. It was inevitable that I would end up dating real-estate salesmen. Invariably, they were tall and handsome, with the gift of the gab, but not exactly the most faithful kind of guy.'

'I see,' Alex said thoughtfully. 'Go on.'

Harriet was glad to see that Alex had lost his disgruntled expression, his blue eyes no longer cold and steely.

'By the time I turned twenty-seven, I decided I was wasting my time on men like that. So I sat down and made a checklist of what I wanted in a husband.'

'A checklist?' he repeated, looking both surprised and amused.

'Find it funny if you like. Emily certainly does.'

'Who's Emily? Your sister?'

'No. Emily's my best friend. She's an English

teacher who flatted with me for a while. It was through her that I met Dwayne.'

'I did wonder how you two met. Frankly, I never thought you were all that well suited. Still, Dwayne must have met your checklist to begin with.'

Harriet sighed. 'I thought he did, till he moved in with me and eventually showed his true colours. I now appreciate that it's impossible to know a man's true character till you live with him. Dwayne certainly met the first three requirements. When I made up my checklist, I decided that I wouldn't even go out with a man till he ticked those three boxes. That way I hoped to avoid falling in love with any more Mr Wrongs.'

Alex's mind boggled over what those three requirements might be. Harriet was right about his finding the idea of a checklist funny. He did. Though he shouldn't have. Didn't he have a checklist of his own when it came to the girls he dated? They had to be in their early twenties, pretty and easy-going. He had a feeling, though, that Harriet's checklist would be a lot more fascinating. And, yes, very funny indeed.

'Do tell,' he said, trying to keep a straight face.

'Promise me you won't laugh.'

'I promise,' he said, but the corners of his mouth were already twitching.

'Okay, well, the first requirement is he can't be too tall or too short. Whilst I find tallness attractive, I've found that too-tall men are often arrogant, whilst too-short men can suffer from the "short man" syndrome.'

Alex realised that at six-foot-four he probably came into the 'too tall' category.

'Do you think I'm arrogant?' he asked.

'A little. But not in a nasty way.'

'Thank God for that. And requirement number two is?'

'He can't be too handsome or too ugly.'

Well, Dwayne had certainly been on the money there. As for himself… Harriet would probably label him in the 'too handsome' category.

'And number three?'

'He can't be too rich or too poor.'

'Right.' Well, that certainly ruled *him* out as a prospective date for Harriet. Not that he would ever ask her out. He'd have to be mad to date Harriet.

But, as he looked into her big brown eyes, Alex was struck by the startling realisation that that was exactly what he wanted to do. Take her out, then take her back to bed.

Bad idea, that, he thought and busied himself stuffing his mouth full of bagel whilst trying to work out where such a potentially self-destructive desire had come from. After all, Harriet didn't fit his own checklist for dating candidates any better than he fitted hers!

Still, it didn't take Alex all that long privately to admit that he'd secretly wanted to take Harriet to bed since the day he'd interviewed her ten months ago. The attraction had been there from the moment she'd walked into his office, looking deliciously nervous but beautifully turned out in a sleek black suit which had followed the curves of her very feminine figure. Her dark brown hair had been up in a professional and somewhat prissy style, but her lushly glossed mouth had betrayed her true nature. He'd immediately made the decision not to hire her, despite her excellent résumé—till he found out she was safely engaged, at which point he'd fooled himself into thinking he could ignore his hormones.

And he had, up till now.

They would have remained in control, too, if she hadn't broken up with Dwayne; if she hadn't cried and he hadn't hugged her. That had been the catalyst which had started the chemical reaction which saw him now being tempted to do something seriously stupid.

Thank God it was still just a temptation. He didn't have to act on it. Didn't have to suffer the humiliation of Harriet rejecting him, not just because he was her boss, but because he was too tall, too handsome *and* too rich.

His sudden laughter brought a reproving look into her velvety brown eyes.

'You promised you wouldn't laugh,' she chided him.

'Sorry. Couldn't help it.'

'In that case, I won't tell you the rest of my checklist. You'd probably crack up entirely.'

'You could be right, there. So I'll save up the rest of your checklist till a later date. Now, I think we should finish up here and get back to work.'

CHAPTER FOUR

HARRIET SIGHED AS she sat back down at her desk and turned on her computer. She hadn't wanted to go back to work; back to reality. She'd been enjoying having coffee with Alex, despite her many *faux pas*. She hadn't really minded his laughing at her checklist, which she now appreciated *was* rather funny. Whilst it did have some merit, such strategies simply didn't work out in real life, just like those silly matchmaking forms they made you filled in on online dating sites.

Most women ended up marrying men they met through work, Harriet accepted, thinking of her other married girlfriends. Actually, *all* her girlfriends were married, a thought which was rather depressing. Harriet was well aware that marriage and motherhood wasn't the only pathway to happiness and fulfilment in life, but it was her chosen pathway. That and a career. Yes, she wanted to have it all, which was possibly where she was going wrong. Having it all suddenly seemed beyond her grasp. This time next year, she'd be hitting thirty. After thirty, finding a husband became more difficult; all the good ones were already snapped up.

Even ordinary men like Dwayne weren't exactly thick on the ground. Maybe she shouldn't have been so quick to dump him. Maybe she should have ignored his failings and accepted him for the imperfect specimen he was...

Harriet was pondering this conundrum when Alex strode out of his office and perched his far too perfect body on the corner of her thankfully large desk.

'A couple of things I forgot to tell you this morning,' he said as he hitched his right knee up into a more comfortable position, indicating he was staying put for a while. 'First, I want you to book me a flight to Milan, arriving on the twenty-ninth of July.'

'Milan?' she echoed, forgetting that it wasn't a PA's job to question her boss, just to obey.

'Yes. Milan, Italy. One of my best friends from Oxford is getting married on the thirty-first. I've been ordered to be there two days before the actual wedding so that I can be attired suitably for my job as best man. The other best man obviously fears I might show up in jeans and a T-shirt.'

Harriet blinked her astonishment at such a ludicrous idea. The night they'd attended that fundraising dinner back in March, Alex had walked into the hotel ballroom wearing a magnificent black tux. He'd quite literally taken her breath away.

'How ridiculous,' she scoffed. 'You are one of the best-dressed men I've ever met.'

'You haven't seen me when I'm slumming it. Jeremy has.'

'Jeremy?'

'The other best man and possibly the best-dressed rake in all of London.'

Harriet's eyes widened. 'Your best friend is a rake?'

'Birds of a feather flock together, you know.'

'You're not a rake,' she defended. 'You just pick the wrong girls to date. The reason they never last is that you get bored with them.'

Alex stared at Harriet and thought how right she was. He did get bored with the women he dated.

But that was exactly what made them safe. They never touched him with any depth of feeling, never moved his soul. Leaving them behind was so damned easy.

The truth hit that he wasn't unhappy with his life so much, but he was bored. Bored with dating silly young girls. Bored with never having a decent conversation with a woman.

He hadn't been bored having coffee with Harriet this morning. He'd been alternately annoyed, then angry, then amused and, yes, aroused. A whole gamut of emotions. He hadn't been able to settle back down to work afterwards; he'd been looking for any reason to come out and talk to her again. Having Harriet book that flight for him had just been an excuse. He could quite easily have done it himself.

I'm not going to be able to resist this attraction, Alex finally conceded, *no matter what the danger*. He suspected she would not reject him; the sexual chemistry which had sprung up today was not all on his side. Alex had noticed her pique when the brunette in the café had flirted with him.

He still hesitated to ask her out on a regular

date, sensing that it was too soon for such a move. Clearly, she was still hurting over the break-up with Dwayne. On top of that, she was his PA, one of the many reasons she'd given to explain why she would never fall in love with him. Not that he wanted her love, just her body. If truth be told, he didn't want Harry to be his next girl-friend. He just wanted to have an affair with her. A strictly sexual affair.

He should have been disgusted with himself. But Alex soothed his conscience by reassuring himself that he would never hurt Harry. He could give her pleasure and fun, something which he suspected had been in short supply in her life for some time.

The only problem was finding a way to achieve his aims without offending her.

An idea struck, one which would sound per-fectly reasonable but which would give him the opportunity to act upon his feelings away from the office. Of course, there was always the risk that Harry would still reject his advances. And, yes, she might even be offended by them. Alex suspected she was a stickler for propriety in the workplace. But it was a risk he was prepared to take. It had been a long time since he'd lived on the edge, so to speak, and it excited him. *She* excited him.

His eyes met with hers, his gaze intense as he searched her face for a sign that he'd been right about her body language when they'd been having coffee together. Alex was gratified when a faint flush bloomed in her cheeks.

'My having to go to Italy for days on end couldn't have come at a worse time,' he said, schooling his own face into a concerned mask. 'I need to be continually hands-on with that golfing estate if it's going to be up and running by Christmas. Someone has to be up there every week to crack the whip. While I'm away, that person will have to be you, Harry.'

'*Me?*' she squawked.

'Yes, *you*,' he insisted. 'I've heard you over the phone to our contractors when they've been giving us grief. You are one tough cookie when you want to be.'

'But doesn't that job already have a foreman in charge?'

'Yes, but even the best foreman can get slack when he's working that far from the boss. If I hadn't been driving up there on a regular basis, we'd be even further behind than we are. I don't want any more delays.'

'Right,' she said, still looking a bit hesitant.

'I thought we could drive up there this Friday, stay overnight, then drive back on the Saturday. We'll stay overnight. And not in some dreary motel, either. Book us a two-bedroomed apartment at a five-star resort in Coffs Harbour. That's only a half-hour drive from the golf course. Somewhere near the ocean, with a balcony and a sea view. And make sure they have a decent restaurant. In fact, we might stay another night, then drive back on the Sunday. You deserve a break after what you've been through.'

CHAPTER FIVE

HARRIET DIDN'T KNOW what to say. She had travelled with Alex only once before. To the Gold Coast, to meet with some Japanese billionaires who'd been staying there at the Hotel Versace and who were potential clients for his new golf resort. But they'd travelled by plane and she'd taken a taxi to the airport by herself. She'd also stayed in a totally separate hotel room. The thought of staying with her way-too-sexy boss in an apartment—for possibly two nights—made her feel… what, exactly?

'Panic' came close to describing her reaction.

Before today, Harriet would have been supremely confident that Alex would never make a move on her. But things were different now. Lisa was past history and so was Dwayne. A new intimacy had sprung up between them, first when Alex had hugged her, and then when they'd had coffee together, an inevitable result once you started opening up about your private life to another person, even when that person was your boss. Harriet knew that men found her attractive. Why should Alex be any different?

And then there was her own silly self. She'd always been blindly attracted to men who were tall, handsome and, yes, super-successful, a failing which she'd worked hard to conquer. But she was in a highly vulnerable state at the moment and, when she faced it, when it came to tall, handsome and super-successful men, Alex was at the top of the heap. To stay with him in an apartment for two nights was asking for trouble.

She didn't need any more trouble in her life. She did, however, need her job; the mortgage on her Bondi apartment barely manageable now that she didn't have anyone to help with the payments. Having an affair with the boss was a sure way to lose her job. Harriet had been around long enough to know how such relationships ended.

'Thank you for your kind offer,' she said in her best businesslike voice. 'But I can't stay away for two nights. Emily is getting back from Bali on Saturday and we're having a catch-up lunch on Sunday.' This was a bald-faced lie. Emily was away for a further two months. Harriet knew, however, that she needed a decent excuse to get out of this. Alex didn't like being told no.

'Pity,' he muttered, then shrugged his shoulders, his indifference indicating he hadn't had any dastardly secret agenda when he'd suggested a two-night stay. He was just trying to be nice to her again. Truly, she was letting herself get carried away here, thinking he had seduction on his mind, a prospect which she had found perversely appealing and painfully flattering. Oh, dear... She seriously wished he'd get off the corner of her desk. Or alternatively stop swinging his foot like that. He was making her way too aware of his body, his very hunky, handsome male body.

Harriet picked up a biro so that she could pretend to take notes and not look at him.

'I'll get onto those bookings right away,' she said. 'I presume you'll be flying first class to Milan?' This with a quick glance his way.

'Of course,' he replied and smiled at her.

When Harriet's heart gave a lurch, she told herself quite fiercely just to stop it. But she might as well have tried to stop the tide from coming in. Why, oh why, did women find men like Alex so damned attractive? She supposed it was a primal thing, the female of the species blindly surrendering to the alpha male because that was the way of nature. But that didn't make it any easier to endure. The last thing she wanted was to start suffering from some silly crush.

'What about a date for the return flight?' she asked crisply.

'Mmm. Can't say I'm sure when that will be. I might spend a day or two with Jeremy in London after the wedding. It's summer over there at the moment. Look, just make it the one-way to Milan. I'll organise the return flight myself when I'm over there.'

'Fine. I'll scout around and see what's the best first-class deal. Might take me a while. First, I'll look up the various five-star resorts at Coffs Harbour,' she went on, putting the biro down and clicking on the computer to bring up resorts at Coffs Harbour. 'Get your tick of approval whilst you're here. Hmm… An ocean view, you said. With a balcony. It *is* winter, you know. I doubt we'll be spending too much time on an ocean-facing balcony.'

'Possibly not,' he agreed. 'But I like apartments with balconies. They're usually larger and have better light.'

'A balcony it is, then. Here's one which should suit—the Pacific View resort just south of Coffs Harbour. They have a two-bedroom spa suite available for Friday night which has a huge balcony with an ocean view.'

'And the other facilities?'

'Everything you could possibly want. There's a heated indoor pool as well as a gym and not one but two restaurants—one a bistro, the other *à la carte*.'

'Great.'

'Shall I book it, then?'

'Absolutely. Oh, and, Harry,' Alex added as he slid off the corner of her desk. *Finally*. 'Perhaps it might be best not to mention where we'll be staying to the rest of the staff, especially Audrey. She might jump to the wrong conclusion, the way she did this morning when she walked in on my hugging you. We don't want to start up any rumours, do we?'

'Absolutely not. Right you are, boss. Mum's the word.'

'Good girl,' he said, before heading back into his office.

Harriet almost laughed. Because all of a sudden she didn't want to be a good girl. She wanted to be a very bad girl. With Alex.

She was in the process of making the bookings when a courier walked in, holding a huge bouquet of assorted flowers.

'Someone's a lucky girl,' he said, smiling a goofy smile. 'The lady on reception said they were for you.'

Harriet's first hideous thought was that they were from Dwayne, in some vain attempt to get her back. But when she opened the card which accompanied the flowers, the words written there brought tears to her eyes for the second time that day.

Hope you're feeling better soon.
Love from Audrey.
PS The bum wasn't good enough for you,
anyway.

The PS made her laugh, which came as a relief to the courier, who was looking worried.

'Everything's fine,' she said to him, waiting till he left before going out to reception and thanking Audrey profusely.

'Flowers always make me feel better,' Audrey said. 'So does a glass of wine or two. Want to come have a drink with me after work?'

'Love to,' Harriet said. She'd missed her girls' nights out with Emily since she'd gone away.

'Great,' Audrey said. 'You should join the rest of us on Friday nights as well.'

'I will in future,' Harriet said. 'But I can't this Friday night. Have to go north with the boss to inspect his new golf resort. He has to go away overseas again soon and he wants me to keep a personal eye on things up there,' she added by way of explanation. 'So I need to see the lie of the land and meet the foreman.'

'That's a long drive. You'll have to stay somewhere overnight.'

'Probably. Still, there are plenty of motels up that way.'

'True.'

'I'd better get back to work or the slave driver might come looking for me.'

'He can be like that, can't he?'

'He's a workaholic, that's for sure.'

'I wouldn't like to do your job.'

'I don't mind. I like it.' An understatement. She *loved* her job.

'Don't you get fed up with being at his beck and call all the time? I mean, the things he asks you to do sometimes.' Audrey rolled her eyes.

Harriet just laughed. Alex had been very upfront at her interview over the menial tasks he might ask her to do. She honestly didn't mind getting his bagels, buying presents for members of his family or even organising his dry-cleaning. Better than sitting at her desk all the time.

It wasn't till Harriet was sitting back down at that same desk that she realised she would enjoy the drive up to the golf estate this weekend very much if she wasn't starting to have these awkward feelings for Alex. Still, at least these days she was capable of resisting such self-destructive desires, having become wise to her own weaknesses where the opposite sex—and sex—was concerned. In time, these feelings would pass and she would meet someone else, someone who could satisfy her in bed and tick at least some of the boxes in her checklist, someone more in her league than the boss of Ark Properties.

The man himself suddenly materialised by her desk.

'So what's with the flowers?' he demanded, his face decidedly grim. 'I hope they're not from your idiot of an ex, trying to get back into your good books.'

'Hardly. They're from Audrey. Wasn't that sweet of her?'

'Very sweet. Look, I have to go out. Family emergency. Hold the fort till I get back.'

Harriet frowned at his swiftly departing back as well as his brusque manner. She wondered what kind of family emergency. He never talked about his family. Yet she knew he had a father still living, and a married older sister who had two children, a boy aged ten and a girl aged eight. She knew because she'd bought Christmas and birthday presents for them.

Maybe she would ask him about his family during the long drive north on Friday. And maybe not.

Friday now loomed in Harriet's mind as a day fraught with unspoken tension. Life, she decided, wasn't being very kind to her at the moment.

But then she looked at Audrey's flowers and smiled.

CHAPTER SIX

IT TOOK ALMOST an hour for Alex to drive from the inner city out to Sarah's home in North Rocks. Sydney's traffic situation was getting worse with each passing year. No matter how many motorways they built, nothing seemed to ease the congestion, or the delays. But the level of his frustration when he finally pulled up outside the house he'd bought his sister some years back was not due to road rage but rage of a different kind.

Gritting his teeth, he jumped out from behind the wheel and stormed through the front gate, bypassing the front door and making his way hurriedly round to the back of the house to the entrance to the granny flat. The one-bedroomed very comfortable flat accommodated his father, his useless, drunken father, whom Sarah had kindly taken in but with whom Alex had totally run out of patience. He'd only come because Sarah had asked him to.

She was waiting for him in the doorway, startling Alex with how much she looked like his mother at around the same age. Both were petite and dark, though with blue eyes. Sarah was like her mother in nature, too, being strong and sensible. Alex loved her a lot and would do anything for her. He wasn't as fond of her husband, Vernon, who seemed to resent the things Alex bought for his family.

Though he'd taken the house, mortgage-free, hadn't he?

Still, Vernon did put up with his less than ideal father-in-law living with them, so he couldn't be all bad. Of course, he continued to benefit financially from the arrangement, Alex paying their rates and electricity.

'Where is he?' Alex asked, his tone sharp.

'On the floor in the bedroom,' Sarah answered, stepping back to let him enter.

The sight of his father sprawled on his back on the rug beside the bed was infinitely depressing. Not just because he was dead drunk but because of the deterioration of this once fine-looking man. Alex had inherited his looks from his father, who'd been a big blond hunk in his younger days. It was no wonder his mother had fallen for him. But there was nothing attractive about him now. Nothing at all.

'Good God,' he said, shaking his head as he stared down at the ruin at his feet. 'Whatever are we going to do with him?'

'It's not his fault, Alex,' Sarah said with her usual compassion. 'He started drinking to forget and now he can't stop. He's an alcoholic. It's a disease. A sickness.'

'Then he should agree to go into rehab.' Alex had lost count of the number of times he'd suggested rehab to his father, but it always fell on deaf ears. 'It's a pity we can't forcibly admit him.'

'I know. But you can't. He has to volunteer to go. Come on, help me lift him up onto the bed. I would have done it myself, but he's just too heavy and I can't afford to hurt my back again.'

Alex frowned. 'You've lifted him up off the floor before?'

'Only once. You were away and I didn't want to ask Vernon.'

'Don't try to lift him again, Sarah. Call an ambulance if you have to.'

Alex scooped his father up off the floor with ease and laid him down on top of the bed. He stirred slightly, making a disgusting snorting sound, before falling back into his drunken stupor, his mouth dropping wide open. His breath was foul. So was his whole body. He needed a bath, sooner rather than later. Then he needed a good talking-to. This situation simply couldn't go on. It wasn't fair to Sarah.

'I have to go to work soon, Alex,' Sarah said, anxiety in her strained face.

Sarah was an oncology nurse, an occupation which she'd decided on after their mother had died at home without too much in the way of nursing. It occurred to Alex that their mother's early and totally unnecessary death had resulted in two of her children choosing careers which they'd hoped would make a difference. Not so his pathetic father, who'd promptly fallen apart. His only decision about the future was to try to drink himself to death.

'You go,' Alex said. 'I'll stay with him.'

'That would be great. Thanks. Look, he honestly can't help it. He does try, you know. Sometimes he doesn't have a drink for weeks. I told him I wouldn't let him around the kids if he was drunk all the time. He even went to AA meetings. But last week was the anniversary of Mum's death. I found him at her graveside crying his eyes out. After that, he went on one of his benders.'

Alex sighed, finally finding some genuine compassion for the man who'd once been a decent enough father, if always a little weak. His mother had been the strength in the family and his father had adored her. He'd called her his soul mate, his rock. She'd always picked him up when he was down. Which was often, his work history not being the best. He'd constantly been made redundant, making money tight in the family. It had been inevitable that when she died he would fall apart.

Watching his father disintegrate over the years had reaffirmed Alex's own decision to steer clear of marriage, as well as avoiding any deeply emotional attachments. Loving a woman obsessively the way his father had loved his mother was not something Alex wanted in his life.

'I'll make sure he has a bath and eats some food,' Alex told his sister. 'And I'll wash those filthy clothes he's wearing. Then I'll do my best to talk to him, see if he'll try rehab. I have some contacts at the Salvation Army. They have some very good rehab places for alcoholics and addicts.'

'Oh, that would be wonderful!' Sarah exclaimed. 'Thank you, darling brother,' she added, coming forward to give him a hug, reminding him of that other hug he'd been involved in earlier that morning.

Sarah hurried off, leaving Alex alone with his father and his thoughts.

But he was no longer thinking about his father. He was thinking about Harriet and the danger of having an affair with a woman who was vastly different from his usual type of bed partner. Not only was she older and more intelligent, she was emotionally vulnerable at the moment. Frankly, Harriet was way more emotional that he would ever have imagined.

The risk he would be taking by sleeping with her was also far greater than he'd originally envisaged. What if she fell in love with him? Even worse, what if he fell in love with her? Hell! What in God's name had he been thinking? Clearly, he hadn't been thinking, not with his brain, anyway. He'd let his hormones take charge, let them cloud his usual good judgment when it came to matters concerning the opposite sex.

There was only one thing to do. He had to forget living on the edge and put Harriet firmly back into the strictly professional PA box which she'd occupied in his head for the past ten months. He actually would have called her and cancelled the trip up north if it wouldn't make him seem like a blithering idiot. He was thankful now that they would be staying in that apartment together for only one night. But, to be on the safe side, he'd put a dampener on his hormones by working out at length in the gym during the next two days. He'd also get out of the office as much as he could. There were several building projects he had underway around Sydney which he could visit. Out of sight was out of mind. By Friday morning, he'd have himself firmly under control again.

His father stirred again, this time opening his

eyes, blinking blearily at Alex for several seconds before groaning.

'You're not going to lecture me again, son, are you?' he said wearily.

'No,' Alex replied in a firm, no-nonsense voice. 'This time, I'm going to tell you what you're going to do, and you're going to do it, whether you like it not.'

'Am I just?'

'Look, if you want to kill yourself, then do the decent thing and do it quickly. Just don't do it slowly in front of your daughter and your grandkids. They deserve better than that.'

'You don't understand,' he blubbered.

'Yeah, I do. Better than you think. You might not realise this, but Mum's death affected the whole family, not just you. You think Sarah and I didn't grieve? We did. But eventually we all moved on, the way Mum would have wanted us to move on.'

His father looked away in shame.

'It's not too late, Dad,' Alex went on, his voice gentler. 'You can beat this thing if you want to. Sarah's going to need you when the kids get older. You could be here when she can't be. Keep an eye on them. Sarah's been good to you. Time for you to be good back to her. Time for you to step up to the plate and be a man.'

Tears sprung into his father's tired blue eyes. 'It's too late.'

'It's never too late,' Alex insisted. 'People can change, no matter how old they are. It won't be easy, but it will work, if you give it a chance. I'll help you, too, if you let me.'

'You're a good son.'

Alex experienced some guilt at this remark. He hadn't been such a good son. Sarah had been the one who'd shouldered most of the burden of looking after their father. He'd just opened his cheque book. But he vowed to do better in future.

'All right,' his father said with a resigned sigh. 'I'll give it a go.'

CHAPTER SEVEN

HARRIET SET HER alarm for five on Friday morning, having made arrangements with Alex to be at his place at six-thirty.

'Take a taxi on expenses,' he'd told her during the very brief appearance he'd made in the office last Wednesday morning, telling her at the same time that he wouldn't be in at all on the Thursday and that she was to use the extra time she would have to give their website a facelift, something she'd been urging him to do for ages. He didn't explain any of his absences, as was often the case with Alex. She suspected it had something to do with his family emergency.

As the taxi sped towards Alex's Darling Harbour address, Harriet pondered again the nature of said emergency. She hoped none of his family was ill.

When the taxi pulled up to the kerb outside Alex's swish-looking apartment block, Harriet paid the fare, then climbed out, taking a few deep breaths as she waited for the driver to get her bag out of the boot. She no longer felt as nervous about this trip as she had the other day, but was not altogether calm. She'd spent an inordinate amount of time last night putting her wardrobe together for the two days, opting for smart casual, though at the last second she'd thrown in a dressy dress, in case Alex wanted to dine at the resort's *à la carte* restaurant.

Of course that had meant adding the right accessories to the growing pile of clothes.

'Going on holidays, love?' the taxi driver asked as he dropped the rather substantial bag by her feet.

'Something like that,' she replied.

'Hope it's somewhere a bit warmer than this,' he said jauntily as he climbed back in behind the wheel and sped off.

It was a bitterly cold morning, Sydney having been blasted by some air off the Antarctic overnight. Still, it would be warmer where they were going. Harriet had chosen to wear stretch black jeans for the drive, teaming them with black ankle boots and a cream cowl-necked jumper made of the softest mohair. She'd thrown on a fawn trench coat to keep out the early morning chill but which she would remove once they were underway. Alex's car was sure to be heated.

Pulling out her phone, she sent him a text to say she'd arrived.

Wait there, he texted back. I'll be right out.

Harriet was shivering by the time Alex pulled up next to her in his black Range Rover. She regretted not wearing a scarf; wearing her hair up was giving her no warmth around her neck.

'Get in,' he said as he jumped out. 'You look cold. I'll see to your bag.'

Harriet tried not to stare at him. But she'd never seen him in casual clothes before. He always wore a suit in the office. He looked great in a suit. In stone-washed grey jeans and a black leather jacket, however, he looked too hot for words. His fair hair was still wet from the shower, the top spiked up a bit, the sides and back clipped short. She liked it that way. It was dead sexy, supplying an added edge to his already macho looks.

Harriet forcibly had to drag her eyes away, her heart alternatively flipping over, then sinking as she wrenched open the passenger door and climbed in.

And there I was, she thought irritably, *imagining I had this attraction under control.*

Hell on earth, thought Alex as he scooped up the bag and threw it in the back.

He'd taken one look at Harriet standing there, staring at him with those big brown eyes of hers, and he'd known for sure that this thing he felt for her wasn't a one-sided attraction. Alex was well versed in recognising the way women looked at him when they fancied him. And Harry fancied him. But possibly not as much as he fancied her. He was a man, after all, and she was seriously fanciable, especially in those sexy jeans and boots.

By the time Alex took his seat behind the wheel, his resolve not to act on the desire Harriet kept sparking in him was very definitely wavering, especially with her betraying her own feelings just now. Of course, his being her boss still created an ethical dilemma. Such relationships were definitely frowned upon, despite being quite common. Not always ideal, however. Inevitably, there came a time when the woman wanted more. Harriet would always want more. He wouldn't be doing her any favours by taking advantage of her, especially at this time in her life when she was on the rebound and emotionally vulnerable.

Hell, hadn't he been through this thought process before?

He'd already made up his mind to steer clear of her and that was what he should do. End of story. *So just be your normal, bossy self and for pity's sake keep your hands off! Then when you get back to Sydney tomorrow night, go out and find yourself a new girlfriend. With a bit of luck, by the time you go to work on Monday your head will be out of your trousers and back on business!*

Harriet forgot about taking off her coat, buckling up the seat belt over it and propping her large black handbag in her lap whilst doing her best to adopt a relaxed facade. But inside, that tension which she'd been fearing was gathering with force, making her jump slightly when Alex gunned the engine.

'You seem to have packed a lot for one night,' he said as he drove off.

Harriet managed a casual shrug of her shoulders. 'I'm never sure what clothes to take, so I always take more than I need.'

'It's a common female trait,' Alex said. 'When I took Hailey to Vanuatu for a long weekend, she had so much luggage I had to pay for extra baggage.'

Harriet had quite liked Hailey. Much better than Lisa. She didn't like any of Alex's girlfriends now, jealousy having raised its ugly head. Lord knew what she would do when the next one came along. And she would. There was nothing surer.

'I'll remember that when you take me to Vanuatu,' Harriet quipped.

Alex laughed. 'You mean you'd settle for Vanuatu? I would have thought Venice was more your style.'

Harriet winced as a memory hit her. 'You know, I wanted to go to Italy for my honeymoon. I'd always wanted to see Rome and Florence and, yes, Venice most of all. Imagine a city built on water! But Dwayne said Italy was overrated and that Bali was just as good. And way cheaper.'

'He sounds like a gem,' Alex said drily.

Harriet snorted. 'Yes, a zircon. Everything about him was false.'

'You're well rid of him. But I have to confess I'm still curious over the other check-points on your list, the boxes Dwayne seemed to tick. At first, that is.'

'Oh, God,' Harriet groaned. 'Can't we just forget that stupid list?'

'Since *you* made that list, Harry, then I doubt it was stupid. Come on, tell your dear old boss all about it.'

She had to smile. The only thing right about that description of himself was the word 'boss'. 'Only if you give me your solemn word this time that you won't laugh.'

'If I do, I give you permission to hit me. Though not whilst I'm driving.'

They'd long passed through the harbour tunnel by then and were making their way towards Chatswood, the traffic growing with each passing minute. Like other big cities, Sydney never really slept.

'Well?' Alex prompted when she didn't say anything.

'Gosh, but you can be dogged at times,' she

said, but smiling. It occurred to Harriet with a degree of surprise that their chatting away like this was making her relax. 'Okay, well, after Dwayne passed the first three boxes, the next one was that my husband-to-be was not to be boring or lazy.'

'Huh! I don't know about lazy, but I found him boring when I met him.'

'Yes, well, the rot was setting in by then. In the beginning, he showed me a good time. As for lazy… He went from sharing the housework and washing my car as well as his to being a couch potato.'

'I can understand how that would annoy someone as fastidious as you.'

Fastidious? Harriet wasn't sure if that was a compliment or a criticism.

'How am I fastidious?' she asked him enquiringly.

'Come now, Harry, you're a perfectionist! You always look great for starters, even at six-thirty in the morning. There's not a hair out of place, your make-up is on and your outfit is perfect for travelling. I'll also bet if I went into your place right now it would be spotless, with your bed made and the washing-up all done. Am I right?'

'Not at all. Yes, the bed is made and the washing-up done, but there's clothes all over my bed and the bulb in my bathroom isn't working. A perfectionist would have had it fixed by now instead of just moving a lamp in there so that I can see.'

'Really? I'm shocked.'

She had to smile. 'You're laughing at me again.'

'Never! Now, back to that fascinating checklist of yours. What comes after lazy and boring?'

'Look, I'm not going to go through every individual point with regard to Dwayne, except to say that he failed them all. I'll just recite the rest of the checklist the way it's written down.'

Alex smiled to himself; she clearly knew the list off by heart. 'My husband-to-be is to be easygoing and generous. He has to treat women as equals. He has to be a lover of animals and children. He has to have friends and interests other than work. He has to have empathy for others, especially those less fortunate than themselves. He has to be able to cook and doesn't think cleaning is beneath him. He has to respect me and trust me and love me and never, ever forget my birthday. And that's about it,' she finished, leaving off the last point which was about sex.

'Wow. That's some list. But what about sex? Don't you care what kind of lover he is?'

Harriet pursed her lips, a slight blush touching her cheeks. Trust Alex to notice that she'd by-passed that topic. She could never get anything past him at work, either.

'Well, naturally he has to satisfy me in bed,' she said, trying not to look as embarrassed as she felt.

'In that case, Dwayne must have satisfied you. At first, anyway?'

'I suppose so,' she said with a sigh. 'He could be quite good in bed when he wanted to be.'

'But not great.'

'No,' she admitted. 'Not great. Look, I don't feel comfortable talking about this,' she went on quite truthfully. The last thing she needed was to start thinking about sex when the object of her desire was sitting right next to her. 'Could we talk about something else? Work, perhaps, or the weather? And could you turn the heating down in this thing? It's very hot in here.'

Alex rarely felt shame, but he did at that moment. Asking Harriet personal questions like that was very definitely crossing the line, especially since he'd resolved not to act on the sexual feelings he'd been having about her. He couldn't help suspecting, however, that her flushed face was not entirely due to his putting the heater up too high.

Talking about sex could sometimes be very arousing, the brain being the most erotic area in the human body. The thought that she was sitting there in a turned-on state was not conducive to resisting temptation.

Gritting his teeth, Alex adjusted the temperature.

'I've turned the heating down,' he said. 'But perhaps you should take that coat off. I've only got a T-shirt on under my jacket, so I feel fine. You look like you've got a very warm jumper on.' And a very sexy-looking one, he'd noted earlier. All soft and furry, the kind you wanted to reach out and touch.

'I meant to take it off earlier,' she said. She was quick, the coat dispensed with in no time and her seat belt snapped back on.

'Throw it over onto the back seat,' he said when she went to lay the coat across her lap.

Alex glanced over at her as she twisted in her seat to do as he said, the movement bringing his attention to the swell of her breasts beneath her jumper. Her very nice breasts. It sent a message to his groin which made him wince.

Damn and blast! It wasn't Harriet who was sitting here in a turned-on state. It was his own stupid self. He should never have asked her about her sex life with Dwayne. He never should have organised this whole fiasco of a trip in the first place!

'I'll put the radio on,' he said brusquely. That way he wouldn't be tempted to ask her any more inappropriate questions. 'Do you want a news and chat channel? Or just music?'

CHAPTER EIGHT

'WHAT?' HARRIET COULDN'T think for a moment, her mind still on that look Alex had given her a moment ago. Had she imagined it or had he stared at her breasts?

Of course you were imagining it, you idiot, came the stern rebuke. *Why would he be ogling your very ordinary C-cups? They can't compare with Lisa's double Ds. Stop focusing on sex and just answer the man.*

'Just music, thanks,' she said, pressing her thighs together tightly in a vain attempt to bring her body under control, her silly, traitorous body which had become all hot and bothered. Talk about pathetic!

'Music,' Alex said to the computerised dash-board and a woman's voice came back with a request for more information. Whilst Harriet was technically savvy, her four-year-old car didn't have such advanced technology. She recalled

Alex saying something about updating his SUV when he'd come back from London recently. So this had to be it.

'What kind of music do you like?' Alex asked her.

Harriet didn't really have a favourite style of music. But she supposed she had to say something. 'Country and Western.'

'Country and Western,' he commanded the computer and almost immediately a song came on that she liked.

'Amazing,' she said. 'You don't even have to insert a flash disc or a CD.'

'It's almost as brilliant as my PA.'

Harriet flushed with pleasure. This was another part of her job she liked—the way Alex would compliment her. Her previous bosses had never done that. Clearly, their fragile male egos had been threatened by her. Not so with Alex. Of course, there was nothing fragile about *his* ego. Or about him. He was a big man in every way.

'You did a brilliant job on our website, by the way,' he went on. 'I had a look at it last night and I was very impressed. It's better laid out and more user-friendly. And I like the way you included photos of the staff. Nothing like the personal touch.'

'That was Audrey's idea,' she admitted, not being one to take credit for something that someone else had suggested. 'We went out for drinks after work on Tuesday, and when I said I was going to revamp the website, she had quite a few excellent suggestions. She's an online shopping addict, so she knows what works and what doesn't.'

'She's a smart lady, Audrey. But inclined to gossip. Did you remember not to tell her we wouldn't be staying up here overnight?'

'Like you just said, Alex, she's smart. Audrey had already concluded we'd be staying somewhere overnight. But I let her think we'd be bunking down in separate rooms in an ordinary motel, not in an apartment at a five-star resort.'

'Good thinking. Did you organise someone to feed the cat while you're away?'

'Yes, Audrey's doing it.'

'That's good. Can't have the poor old thing passing away from starvation while we're away. You'd blame me, and I don't think I could live with the guilt.'

'Don't be silly. You have nothing to feel guilty about where Romany is concerned. Did I ever thank you for letting him be the office cat?'

'Only about a hundred times.'

'Oh. Yes, well, it was still very good of you. Poor Romany,' she said with a sigh. 'I dare say he'll die soon. Still, at least we made the last part of his life a little happier.'

'You do spoil him rotten, Harry. Sometimes I almost feel jealous of that cat. Now, I don't want to stop again till we get to Port Macquarie, probably around eleven. I want to make the golf estate by two o'clock at the latest. Is that all right with you?'

'That's fine,' she agreed.

'If you need a break before then, just say so.'

'I'll be all right.'

'Good. Now, just settle back and relax and listen to the music. Eventually, though, I'll have to make some business calls. But not yet. It's still early.'

Harriet doubted that she would relax, but amazingly she did, the heated seats and the music melting away her earlier tension. She even drifted off to sleep, jolting awake when Alex started talking more loudly than the music. She listened, amazed at how much he could achieve on the phone in just a couple of hours, contacting all the foremen on his current building projects, demanding updates on their progress, giving them a hurry-up when needed.

Eleven saw them eating a disgustingly fattening lunch in the service centre near the turn-off to Port Macquarie, Alex scoffing at her comment that she'd end up with a backside the size of a bus if she ate that for lunch every day.

'No worries there, Harry. You would starve rather than eat this kind of food every day.'

'True,' she agreed.

'It doesn't hurt to bend your rules every once in a while, you know.'

She stared at him across the wooden bench, wondering what rules he was referring to. Probably that silly checklist of hers. Not that all of it was silly. In fact, a lot of those rules made perfect sense. The trouble was that men weren't perfect, so finding someone to fit all her far-too-many requirements was doomed to failure. All she could hope for was that the main ones might be fulfilled. The ones about love and respect and money and, yes, sex.

'You could be right, there,' she mused.

'I *am* right,' he pronounced. 'Now, drink up that cappuccino. Time to get going.'

He was back on the phone again as soon as they hit the road, chatting away with the sales team in the office, finding out how things were going and how many sales they'd had off their various plans. They had several blocks of units in a developmental stage, all of them in the far western suburbs and very reasonably priced. Most were likely to be sold before a single brick was laid. They also had a housing estate near where the new Sydney airport was to be built, which was proving popular with first-time buyers and builders. Harriet listened as Alex told each of the boys personally about his having to go away the week after next. When he finally finished talking, Harriet turned to glance his way.

'By the way, will *we* be handling the sales of the housing blocks on the golf estate, or are you going to give that job to local real-estate agents?'

'Both. And we'll advertise extensively online. That will be *your* job, Harry. Perhaps you can think about that while I'm away, since you won't be running around all the time getting your boss bagels and doing myriad other jobs which the lazy so-and-so could possibly do himself.'

Harriet laughed. 'I don't mind, really.'

'I know you don't. You are indispensable to me, Harry.'

'No one is indispensable, Alex.'

'You are to me. As selfish as it sounds, I'm almost glad that you've broken off your engagement. The thought of you getting married and leaving me to become a mother was filling me with dread.'

Harriet rolled her eyes. What a hopeless exaggerator he was! But, yes, it *was* selfish of him to say that. And rather insensitive.

'Sorry,' she said. 'But I still intend to get married and have at least one baby, so you'll just have to cope when that day comes. But don't worry. I have no intention of giving up my day job just because I'm pregnant. I'll waddle into the office right up to the last second. You might even have to drive me to the maternity ward if my husband is unavailable,' she added with a straight face.

CHAPTER NINE

ALEX WAS HORRIFIED at the thought, plus the image of Harry waddling into the office at some future date with a huge baby bump. He could see it now. Her desk would be littered with magazines that told you everything you needed to know about pregnancy and motherhood—plus everything you didn't need to know. She and Audrey would talk babies *ad infinitum*, spending every lunch hour buying baby clothes, not to mention oodles of those hideous stuffed toys. And, yes, there would be a bag packed and sitting in the corner, ready for the emergency of her suddenly going into labour.

'That won't be happening,' he ground out. 'Audrey can take you in a taxi.'

Harriet laughed. 'You should see your face. What's the problem, Alex? You're not afraid of babies, are you?'

'Immensely. They're noisy and messy and have

no concept of doing what they're told.' He'd visited Sarah once or twice when she'd had newborns and had hardly slept a wink, what with the crying all night. It certainly wasn't something he craved for himself.

'No wonder you've stayed a bachelor if that's what you think.'

'It's what I think. Now, tell me what you think.'

'About what? Babies or bachelors?'

'No. About your surrounds. We're here.' And he pulled over to the side of the road and turned off the engine.

They were on the crest of a hill. Harriet's head swivelled round as she took in the land which would one day be an eighteen-hole golf course surrounded by privately owned homes and some holiday apartments. There would be a well-appointed club house, of course, as well as a small chapel with a lovely garden where weddings could be held. Big money in weddings, Alex had told her during the planning stage.

The land, she knew, had once been a banana plantation that had gone bust when the trees had developed some kind of fungus. A would-be entrepreneur had snapped it up for a bargain price, clearing the land before he himself had gone broke when his financing had fallen through and the stock market had crashed. Alex had stepped in, and here they were today.

She climbed out so that she could have a better look, standing on the grass verge with her hands on her hips whilst assembling her thoughts. The golf course itself looked nearly finished, but the buildings were still at the foundation stage, the rain obviously having held up that part of the project.

'Well?' Alex said as he came to stand beside her.

'It's going to be great. I love the artificial lakes. And the trees. But it's never going to be finished by Christmas,' she added.

Alex frowned. 'You're probably right. God, but I hate it when the weather works against me.'

'You can't control the weather, Alex.'

'I don't seem to be able to control anything much these days,' he muttered.

And then it happened. He turned towards her and she saw it in his eyes—the very thing that she thought she'd imagined this morning. But she wasn't imagining this. The desire—no, the *hunger*—glittering in his sky-blue eyes was very real. Her hands slipped from her hips as she stared back at him, her heartbeat quickening.

Part of her didn't want him to want her like this. It would make Alex like all the other too-tall, too-handsome, too-successful men she'd slept with in the past. But there was no denying what he wanted, his hot gaze coveting her the way the big, bad wolf had coveted those three plump little pigs.

Unfortunately, Harriet knew she wouldn't prove to be the sensible pig who'd built his house out of bricks. She was the silly pig who'd built his house out of straw. One puff and it had fallen down.

Or one kiss, as it turned out.

He didn't say a word as he strode over and pulled her into his arms, all her defences dissolving well before his lips met hers. Her eyes closed as she lifted her mouth and her arms, sliding them up around his neck, pulling him close, her breasts flattening against his chest. Harriet could not recall a kiss affecting her as much as this kiss from Alex. Her head swirled as passion erupted within her like a volcano, her mouth gasping open. His arms tightened around her and his tongue delved deep.

Harriet had been kissed many times before— and by men who were good kissers. But Alex kissing her was something else entirely. His tongue moved back and forth in her mouth, then up, rubbing over the sensitive surface of her palate. She moaned with pleasure and excitement. She didn't want him ever to stop. She loved the way his hands started roaming over her back, sliding up and down her spine. One hand finally settled like a collar around the nape of her neck whilst the other splayed over her bottom, pressing her firmly against his erection. It blew her mind, just how hard he was.

The loud tooting of a horn plus some raucous catcalls had Alex wrenching away from her, his breathing ragged as he glowered at the passing car full of teenagers. Her eyes had flown open with the shock of his abandoning her so abruptly, leaving her still panting and flushed with heat.

'Damn,' he muttered, running his hands agitatedly through his short fair hair whilst scooping in several deep breaths. Shaking his head, he spun away from her, striding over to stand on the edge of the hill, his legs spread wide, his fists balled by his sides.

Harriet stayed where she was, staring over at him, dazed and more than a little shaken. It wasn't every day that she ached to have sex with a man within moments of their first kiss. Not that this was just any man, of course. This was Alex, her boss.

After staring down at the valley for several seconds, he whirled back to face her once more, though still keeping his distance.

'That shouldn't have happened,' he ground out. 'I never meant for that to happen.'

'No,' she said. Harriet didn't imagine for one moment that he had. 'Why did you do it, then?'

His laugh was very dry. 'Come now, Harry, don't play the ingénue with me. You've been around. You know how this works. If truth be told, I've been wanting to do that since the first day you walked into my office.'

Harriet blinked. 'What? You mean at my interview?'

'Yes, at your interview. Even then, I had some misgivings. But I fooled myself into thinking I could keep my hands off. I've never been partial to pursuing women who were in love with someone else, no matter how attractive I found them.' He dragged in a deep breath, then let it out slowly, his expression self-mocking. 'But fate conspired against me this week. I broke up with Lisa and you broke up with Dwayne. If I hadn't hugged you, then taken you out for coffee, none of this would ever have happened. I certainly wouldn't have organised for us to be alone like this.'

The meaning behind his last words took a few seconds to sink into Harriet's somewhat scattered brain, any flattery she'd been experiencing over his confessed attraction soon obliterated by shock.

'Are you saying that this so-called business trip was a deliberate ploy on your part to seduce me?' She'd imagined it might be for a brief moment earlier in the week, before dismissing the idea as ludicrous. 'You never really needed me to oversee this estate while you're away, did you?'

Alex shrugged his broad shoulders. 'No, I didn't need you to oversee this estate for me while I was away—and, yes, it was just an excuse to get you alone. Though I'm not keen on the word "seduce".'

'What else would you call it?' she threw at him angrily. 'You know full well I would never *want* to have an affair with you. You're my boss!'

'You didn't mind my kissing you just now,' he reminded her with brutal honesty. 'But all that is beside the point. I saw the folly of my ways in time and changed my mind about trying to *seduce* you, since you seem to like that word. Perhaps because it stops you from taking any responsibility over what just happened.'

'*You* kissed *me*, Alex. I didn't do a thing!'

'Nothing except look so deliciously sexy this morning that I haven't been able to think of anything else but making love to you all day.'

An already flustered Harriet homed in on his patently false words.

'You don't want to make love to me at all,' she snapped. 'You want to have sex with me. That's a totally different scenario.'

'True,' he said before walking slowly back towards her. 'But nothing changes the fact that we can't go back to the way it was between us, Harry. You want me as much as I want you. Don't deny it,' he said, close enough now to reach out and place his large hands on her suddenly trembling shoulders.

Harriet somehow found her tongue, despite it lying thick and dry in her parched mouth. 'That doesn't mean I have to do anything about it.'

'True again. But why deny yourself something which can give you pleasure? And I can give you pleasure, Harry,' he murmured, his right hand lifting off her shoulder to trace circles around her gasping lips. 'Lots of pleasure.'

'I didn't realise that you could be this wicked,' she choked out.

'There's nothing wicked about sexual pleasure, Harry,' he said, his bedroom-blue eyes going all smoky with desire. 'And there's nothing wrong with our having a sexual relationship, provided we keep it out of the office.'

He could say that, but she knew that if she did this—and her body was screaming at her to surrender—it might eventually cost her her job. Harriet knew of other women who'd had affairs with their bosses and they never came out on top. Never!

But her days of being weak where men were

concerned was over. Harnessing every bit of backbone that she possessed, she stepped back, far enough to force his hand to drop away from her mouth and her still-burning lips. Her action surprised him, which made her smile a wry smile.

You don't know what you're dealing with where I'm concerned, Alex. But you'll learn.

'You're right,' she said crisply. 'About everything. But if we're going to have an affair, then I must set some rules.'

'Rules?' he echoed, his brows lifting skywards.

'Yes, rules.'

His rueful smile annoyed her, but she didn't let it show. She kept her cool and her resolve. Amazing, really, considering what she was about to do. Dwayne had been a big mistake, but Dwayne didn't have the power to hurt her as much as Alex could. Harriet had a history of falling madly in love with men like Alex. No matter how careful she was, it would probably still happen. But no way would he ever know that. The moment she felt even a smidgeon of love for him, her resignation would be on his desk.

'Shoot,' he said.

Harriet scooped in a calming breath before letting it out slowly. 'As you yourself said,' she began, her voice wonderfully cool and steady, 'there will be no sex in the office. That's a definite no-go. But also not during office hours. No sneaking out at lunchtime to some nearby hotel room.'

Alex scowled. 'Sounds like you've been down this road before.'

She hadn't, never having indulged in a secret affair before. All her relationships had been out in the open. But she wasn't about to tell Alex that. 'Like you said earlier, Alex, I've been here before.'

'Any other rules?' he asked, still sounding irritated.

'Only the obvious ones. You will use a condom at all times.' She'd stopped taking the pill after breaking up with Dwayne. 'Also, whilst I'm sleeping with you, you don't sleep with anyone else. The day you take up with a new girlfriend, our relationship—such as it is—will be over.'

'Fair enough. Am I allowed any rules of my own?'

Harriet was taken aback. She hadn't anticipated this. 'But of course,' she said coolly.

'We will not have sex at all during the working week,' he surprised her by saying. 'When I work, I work hard. I can't afford to be wrecked the next day after being up half the night. But I expect you to spend every weekend with me. At my apartment,' he added. 'Starting from Friday night straight after work.'

A highly erotic thrill rippled through Harriet at the thought that he would want her that much. The prospect of spending every weekend at Alex's sexual beck and call was intoxicatingly exciting. She had no doubt he would be good in bed. No, he would be better than just good. He'd be fantastic. All of a sudden Harriet found it hard to concentrate on what she should be saying. But she had to. Her pride demanded it.

'Sorry,' she said crisply. 'No can do. I'll be going out for drinks on a Friday night with friends. I can't get to your apartment till much later in the evening.'

'No problem. I can wait. Waiting sometimes makes it better.'

Harriet suppressed a groan. She really was out of her league here. Yes, she'd had lovers before, but none quite like Alex. She could see that he was very experienced at playing erotic games. But there was no turning back. She wanted him too much.

'I also might have to go out with Emily on the odd Saturday night,' she added, determined to make at least some show of independence.

'Can't you have your girls' night out during the week?'

'Sometimes, but not always. But back to the weekends. What do you mean by "at your apartment"? Aren't you ever going to take me out somewhere? For a drive, perhaps? Or to dinner, or to a show?'

'No. You're my PA, Harriet,' he added, showing her he meant business when he called her Harriet like that. 'You're also a marrying kind of girl. I don't want you to ever think that our affair has anything to do with love. It's about sex and sexual pleasure. It won't last. Maybe only a few weeks. But, let's face it, after what you've been through with Dwayne, you can afford a few weeks to indulge yourself in a purely selfish and strictly sexual relationship.'

Shock rippled through Harriet at the mention of Dwayne. Because she hadn't given him a second thought. The penny dropped that she hadn't been in love with Dwayne for a long time.

No, be honest, Harriet. You were never *in love with him. Yes, it was upsetting breaking up with him. But your heart wasn't broken, just your dreams.*

'When you're ready to move on,' Alex was saying, 'then just say so and we'll call it quits. Okay?'

Harriet just stared at him, stunned by the ruthlessness of his proposal and by her reaction to it. Sheer, unadulterated excitement. It was a struggle to stop the heat inside her body from reaching her face. Somehow, she managed.

'Okay?' he repeated, his eyes narrowing on hers.

'Okay,' she agreed, already afraid that calling it quits might prove impossible. Or it would whilst she was working for him. No matter what happened between them, it was perfectly clear that her days at Ark Properties were now numbered.

'Good,' he said, just a tad smugly. 'I'd kiss you to seal the deal, but I don't dare. After that last kiss, we'd probably end up having sex on the grass and, as much I occasionally fancy a quickie in the great outdoors, I prefer the comfort of a bed. Or a sofa. Or even a nice, warm spa bath.'

Harriet tried to banish the thought of having sex with Alex tonight in the spa bath, but it refused to go, evoking images which both aroused and tormented her. Dear God, but she could hardly wait!

'Now, we'd better get down there and pretend to do some work. I don't want Wally to think I made up some feeble excuse just so I could go away for a dirty weekend.'

But that's exactly what you did, Harriet thought dazedly as they both climbed back into the Range Rover. She didn't believe Alex's claim that he'd changed his mind about seducing her. He'd meant to have her all along. And now, he had her. Game, set and match!

CHAPTER TEN

ALEX STRUGGLED TO keep his focus on the job at hand in the two hours they spent with Wally, though he doubted the foreman noticed. He was too busy chatting away with Harriet and showing her everything. Wally seemed inordinately pleased that she would be visiting him in a couple of weeks' time, and not Alex. It seemed foolish to feel jealousy, but he did.

Alex might have worried about this uncharacteristic reaction more if his head hadn't been projecting forward to the evening ahead. He was impatient to have Harry in his arms again. Impatient to show her that he was the boss, even in the bedroom; that her ridiculous penchant for rules didn't apply to him. Yes, he would always use a condom. He wasn't a fool. But other than that he would not be dictated to, especially when she wanted him as much as he wanted her. He almost felt sorry for Dwayne. How could any man live up to that ridiculous checklist of hers? He'd have to be a saint.

Alex wasn't a saint. Not even remotely. But neither was he cruel or heartless. He was well aware that Harriet had just been through a tough time in her life. But he had no intention of hurting her. Hell, he would never hurt any woman, especially not Harry, whom he respected and admired enormously. Alex felt confident that having an affair with him would actually be good for her. It might encourage her to lighten up a bit. To live for the moment. To just have fun for a while.

By the time they left for the relatively short drive to the nearby resort, Alex had convinced himself that a strictly sexual affair with him was just what the doctor ordered for someone suffering over the break-up of a relationship.

Harriet didn't feel like chatting on the way to the resort, tension over the night ahead gathering in the pit of her stomach. Alex did his best to engage her in conversation, not very successfully. When he finally gave up asking her what she now saw as futile questions about the golf estate, she turned her head to gaze through the passenger window at her surrounds, noting idly that the countryside was very beautiful, with rolling hills and lush paddocks, the grass very green despite it being winter. Not many frosts this far north, she thought. Not to mention near the coast.

A sign came up saying that Coffs Harbour was only a few kilometres away.

By the time they turned into the resort, her nerves were jangling and her belly was as tight as a drum. Harriet still found it hard to believe that she was about to spend the night with Alex. *All* night, in his bed. Maybe even in his bath as well. It stunned her how quickly she had gone from engaged woman to suddenly single to her boss's secret mistress. Not that they'd actually done the deed yet. But it was a foregone conclusion. With the wild desires that were flooding her body at that moment, she couldn't have changed her mind even if she'd wanted to.

The resort was everything its website promised—several storeys high, the main building sat on a bluff overlooking the ocean. It faced north-east, with the back nestled into the rocky hillside. When they pulled into reception shortly after six, the sun had just set and dusk had arrived. Solar-powered lights were on everywhere, lining the circular driveway and winking in the tropical-style gardens. A parking valet descended on them as soon as Alex pulled up, taking care of their luggage while they went inside to book in.

Harriet was slightly taken aback when Alex told her to sit down whilst he handled everything. She was used to doing everything for him, but of course they were no longer just boss and employee; they were about to become lovers. She was glad to sit, her knees going to jelly at the thought.

The foyer was spacious and luxurious, with various seating arrangements dotted around. Over in a far corner was a bar and beyond that a large doorway with a sign over it, indicating the bistro-style restaurant she'd read about. She knew the *à la carte* restaurant was on the top floor, where the view of the ocean would be perfect during the daytime, as well as in the evening in summer, when daylight-saving time had it staying light till eight-thirty. She started thinking this would be the perfect place for future clients of their golf course to stay. She might contact the manager at a later date and see about their advertising on the Ark Properties website.

No sooner had Harriet thought that when she remembered she would probably not be working for Ark Properties for much longer. She sighed, then glanced over at where Alex was still at the desk, booking them in. Would it all be worth it? she wondered. Would the pleasure he'd promised live up to her expectations?

Harriet only had to recall the intoxicating expertise of his kiss to know the answer to that. Sex with Alex was going to be fantastic. Fantastic and unforgettable. It was the unforgettable part, however, which was the real worry. She couldn't imagine herself getting over him as quickly as she'd got over Dwayne. But when Alex turned from the desk and smiled over at her, all her concerns for the future fled. Her heart lurched as she watched him walk towards her. God, but he was gorgeous. Gorgeous and all hers. For now, anyway. Adrenaline shot through her veins, accompanied by the heat of a desire so strong that she wasn't sure she would be able to stand up.

'All done,' he said, still smiling. 'Our luggage has been sent up and they booked us a table for dinner at seven-thirty. Are you coming?' he said and held his hand out.

She put her much smaller hand in his large one, sucking in sharply when his fingers closed hot and strong around hers. He drew her up onto her feet, his mouth no longer smiling, his eyes darkening as they met hers.

'I'm not going to be able to wait till after dinner,' he said in a low, gravelly voice only she would hear. 'This is getting beyond bearing.'

'Yes,' she agreed, her face flushing wildly as everything she'd ever believed about herself was tipped on its head. She'd thought she knew how this kind of thing felt. She'd experienced sexual desire before. But this was different from *anything* she'd ever experienced.

'Don't say another word,' he growled and steered her hurriedly towards the bank of lifts against the back wall. 'When we get into the apartment, I want you to go to your bathroom and shower,' he told her on the way. 'I'll do the same in mine. Don't dress. Just put on one of their bathrobes. We'll meet in the living room. You have ten minutes. Not a second longer.'

There was another couple waiting to use the

lifts and a fiercely aroused Harriet avoided their eyes. But she noticed when the woman started staring at Alex. It used to amuse Harriet when women ogled her boss, but this time she hated it with a passion, especially since this woman was young and attractive. Harriet knew she would have to get a grip on her jealousy if she was to survive her affair with Alex. He wasn't the type of man who'd appreciate a possessive lover.

She kept her eyes averted as they rode the lift upwards, the other couple alighting well before their own stop. Thank God. When the lift doors opened on their floor, Alex took her elbow and ushered her along the hallway.

The apartment was exactly as it had appeared on the website. Harriet already knew the floor plan by heart. The decor was no surprise, either, the website having detailed photos of all the rooms. The furniture was typical five-star-hotel furniture, comfy and classy. The colour palette was in blue, grey and white, the walls white, the carpet grey, the kitchen and bathrooms white.

Harriet didn't stop to look around, though she did notice that Alex actually had more luggage then she had, all their bags having been brought up and deposited in the entrance hall. She swept up her bag and walked swiftly through the living room and down the short hallway into the second bedroom, which she already knew had an *en suite* bathroom. Dropping her bag at the foot of the bed, Harriet raced into the bathroom, stripped off, then plunged into a hot, though far from relaxing, shower.

Harriet was way beyond relaxation. Alex had used the words 'beyond bearing' downstairs. She had already reached that point herself, her mind constantly filling with arousing images, her body balancing on a knife-edge of desire so sharp that the beating of the hot water against her erect nipples was actually painful. When she went to wash between her thighs, she had to stop for fear that she might come.

She was close. So very close. She had to stop thinking about Alex. Had to stop thinking about doing it with him. Had to stop *thinking*. Oh, God…

Harriet snapped off the shower and almost fell out of the cubicle, drying herself inadequately before drawing on the thick white bathrobe that was hanging on the back of the door. A quick glance in the bathroom mirror showed pink cheeks and messed-up hair. Sighing, she took her hair down, combing it with her fingers till it fell around her face in its usual tidy curtain. There seemed little point in bothering with make-up, though a quick spray of deodorant might be a good idea. So would cleaning her teeth. Dashing back into the bedroom, she pulled out her toilet bag and returned to the bathroom to attend to both matters.

More than ten minutes had definitely passed by the time she forced her jelly-like legs to carry her towards the bedroom door, her uncharacteristic tardiness not helped by a new and rather undermining train of thought. As much as she wanted Alex, she was suddenly terrified of somehow disappointing him. Maybe he would find her body too...well...ordinary. She didn't have spectacular breasts, an overly curvy bottom or legs that went up to her armpits. Her figure was very nice— she looked quite good naked—but it was nothing out of the box.

And then there was the worry about her own performance in bed. She'd never had any complaints before, but she suspected that Alex's standards were very high, and very demanding. He'd already demonstrated dominant tendencies, his rules for their affair clearly trying to turn her into some kind of submissive. And, whilst Harriet found such a scenario exciting, she wasn't sure how long she could sustain such a role. It went against her basic nature. Harriet was very independent in spirit, an organiser and a planner. Over the years she'd developed firm ideas over what she wanted in men and in life. Dwayne had gone as far as to call her bossy and controlling during their last argument, but Harriet didn't see herself that way.

Well, maybe a little…

It crossed her mind that her rather scandalous behaviour today could be her subconscious trying to break out of her usual sensible mould by doing something wild and rebellious.

Becoming the boss's secret mistress would certainly qualify as that!

CHAPTER ELEVEN

ALEX GLANCED UP when she entered the living room, his hands stilling on the bottle of champagne he was opening. It had been sitting in an ice bucket on the kitchen counter, along with two champagne glasses and a basket of fruit. Compliments of the management.

It had been over ten minutes since she'd fled his presence like the hounds of hell were after her. Her big brown eyes, he noted, looked just as they had that day he'd interviewed her. Deliciously nervous yet fiercely determined at the same time. He wondered how they would look when she was about to come. Would they grow wider, or scrunch up as she struggled not to let go?

He liked to prolong a woman's pleasure. Liked to prolong his own as well. Alex suspected, however, that there wouldn't be much prolonging this first time.

'Do you like champagne?' he asked.

She blinked, then stared at the bottle, as though she hadn't even seen it.

'Not really,' she replied. 'It gives me a headache.'

Alex laughed, then dumped the bottle back in the ice bucket. 'Well, we can't have that, can we? Should I make you some coffee, then? You must be thirsty.'

'I don't want anything,' she said before sucking in a deep breath. 'Just you.'

Harriet's bold admission shocked her. And him as well, judging by the startled look on his face.

But she simply hadn't been able to bear the thought of any more delay.

His surprised expression soon changed to one of hunger, his blue eyes clouding as they narrowed, then focused on her mouth.

She just wanted his hands on her naked body, and him inside her.

When he came out from where he'd been standing behind the breakfast bar, Harriet froze, needing all of her physical and mental strength to hold herself upright as he walked towards her. When he was close enough, he reached out and slowly

undid the sash of the robe, Harriet's chest tightening as he parted it. When he slipped his hands
inside and started playing with her tightly aching
nipples, she gasped, then groaned. As much as
she craved such attention, she craved him more.

'Please don't torture me, Alex,' she said shakily, her desperate eyes pleading with him.

'Don't torture *you*!' he exclaimed, then laughed.
'Sweetheart, you've been torturing me all day.'
After shoving the ice bucket down to one end of
the counter, he took a rough hold of her waist and
hoisted her up onto the stone breakfast bar, pushing her back till her upper body was flat, parting
her robe further, then parting her legs.

She could feel the cold of the stone counter
through the robe, but she wasn't cold. Not at all.
Harriet watched, eyes wide, as he moved to stand
between her outspread legs, her head lifting a little when he unwound the sash on his own robe.
She wanted to see him. Wanted to watch him.

Her mouth dried at the sight of his erection. He
was even bigger and harder than she'd imagined.
And already sheathed with a condom.

'No, don't!' she cried out when he rubbed the

tip against her clitoris, her nerve-endings already on the edge of release. 'Just do it.'

He swore, Harriet's head clunking back onto the bench top with relief when he pushed himself into her. Her relief was short-lived, however, as the dizzying pleasure of his possession was rapidly eclipsed by the speed and strength of the most intense orgasm she'd ever experienced. Spasm followed spasm, the sensations electrifying. Her mouth fell open as she dragged in a much-needed breath, her eyes closing when the room began to spin. They flew open again when Alex suddenly grabbed her hips, holding her captive with an iron grip as he came, his sex pulsating violently in tandem with her own contractions. Their mutual climax went on for ages, sating Harriet with the most overwhelming waves of pleasure.

Finally, their bodies grew still and calm, leaving Harriet lying there staring dazedly up at the ceiling whilst she struggled to gather her thoughts. For this was what she'd feared—a pleasure, a satisfaction, so out there that it would have her coming back for more, long after it wasn't wise. Hopefully, she wouldn't fall in love with Alex.

Hopefully, she could keep it at just lust, or infatuation, or whatever this kind of sexual obsession was called. Already she was looking forward to those weekends where he wanted her to be at his sexual beck and call. There was nothing she wouldn't do for him. Nothing!

His lifting her up from the counter to hold her tenderly against him brought a moan of dismay to her lips. She didn't want tenderness from him. She just wanted sex. Alex might be able to indulge in tender post-coital embraces without letting his emotions get involved, but Harriet wasn't of that ilk. She would have to put a stop to such hypocritical nonsense before disaster struck. After all, *he* was the one who said he just wanted a strictly sexual relationship. An affair, not a *love* affair. Which was exactly all *she* wanted from him. Clearly, he needed reminding of that fact.

Alex was taken aback when Harriet pulled back out of his arms.

'Wow,' she said as she lifted her hands to finger-comb her hair. 'I obviously needed that.'

Her remark sent Alex's teeth clenching down hard in his jaw. He hated to think that her urgent responses to him were the result of nothing but an intense sexual frustration. He preferred to believe she found him as attractive and desirable as he found her. He didn't like her implying that she was just scratching an itch with him. Surely she was just trying to find excuses for coming so quickly? Not that he cared. He'd come pretty quickly himself. And it had felt fantastic. Frankly, he hadn't had an orgasm that intense in living memory. Their coming together had helped, of course. God, the way she'd gripped his erection had been amazing. He could not wait to feel that again.

But he would have to wait, he supposed. They really should be getting dressed for dinner. But he was still inside her, damn it. And he wanted seconds.

Without asking, he slid his hands under her bottom and scooped her up off the counter. Thank God she was just a light little thing, but it still wasn't the most comfortable position with her legs dangling by her sides.

'What do you think you're doing?' she gasped, grabbing the lapels of his robe before thankfully wrapping her legs around him.

'That was a very nice entree, Harry,' he told her as he turned and carried her towards the main bedroom. 'But not nearly enough for me. My sexual appetite runs to five-course meals.'

He loved the wild glittering in her dilated eyes. She wanted seconds as much as he did.

'Don't worry,' he went on. 'We'll stop after the second course and save the rest till after we've eaten some real food. Nothing like a break to whet the appetite again.'

CHAPTER TWELVE

IT WAS AFTER seven-thirty by the time an elegantly dressed Alex steered a somewhat shell-shocked Harriet into the restaurant for dinner. Thankfully, she didn't look as shattered as she felt. The designer dress she was wearing, which had cost her a week's wages, fitted her figure like a glove, the emerald colour complementing her dark hair. Her make-up was perfect and her black patent leather bag matched her shoes, their four-inch heels giving her some much-needed height, especially when she was with Alex, who easily ticked her 'too tall' box.

Harriet did her best to exude an air of cool sophistication as their waiter showed them to their table. But it was a struggle to put aside the memories of what had just transpired. Less than twenty minutes earlier she had been stark naked in Alex's shower, her hands outstretched on the wet tiles, every muscle in her body tight as a drum as he teased her endlessly with a soapy sponge, then took her from behind, her moans muffled by the hot jets of water streaming over her back. She'd come quickly again, but Alex hadn't. He'd lasted and lasted and, astonishingly, when he'd finally come, so had she. Which was a first for her. She'd never come twice like that. Not in such a short space of time. Yet perversely, as soon as he'd withdrawn, she'd found herself wanting more. Before she'd been able to stop herself, she'd spun round and grabbed him, kissing him passionately.

It was Alex who'd put a stop to proceedings. Harriet flushed at the memory of his smacking her on the bottom and telling her not to be so greedy; that it was time to dress for dinner and she would just have to wait.

Harriet sucked in a deep breath as she sat down, the position reminding her that she was still on the sensitive side down there. Not sore, exactly. Just…sensitised. Feeling perversely embarrassed—really, what was there to be embarrassed about?—Harriet reached for the white linen serviette, flicking it open and placing it across her lap before the waiter did it for her.

'What would you like to drink?' Alex asked, forcing her to glance across the table at him.

Hopefully, her gaze was cooler than her cheeks. 'Something white and dry. But not too dry. I'll probably order seafood.'

'My thoughts exactly,' he replied, then handed the drinks menu to the hovering waiter, telling him to bring their best bottle of Verdelho.

'You trust him to pick for you?' she asked after the waiter hurried off.

'Why not? It's his job. I've never been a serious wine buff. I also don't drink much any more. I used to during my Oxford days—but I didn't have to pay for the wine at the time,' he added with a rather odd little smile.

'Why's that?'

'It's a long story. I might tell it to you one day, but not tonight. Tonight I want to find out a little more about you.'

'Me?'

'Yes, you, Harriet McKenna. So, tell me… what's your story? Before Dwayne, that is. I think I've heard enough about dear old Dwayne.'

Harriet pressed her lips tightly together. She really didn't want to open up any further to

Alex. She'd already told him more than he needed to know.

'It's all in my résumé,' she said.

'Ah,' Alex said with a drily amused smile. 'You've decided to play the mysterious *femme fatale*, have you?'

Harriet shook her head at him. 'I'm not playing at anything, Alex. I'm simply keeping to the rules we set down when we started this strictly sexual affair. We don't need to know each other's life stories to have sex. In fact, telling each other all our past histories could be counterproductive. Exchanging confidences and secrets brings on emotional involvement. I don't want that. And neither do you.'

Absolutely not, Alex accepted. But, damn it all, he was curious about her. He suspected for the first time that there was a lot more to Harriet than he'd read in her résumé.

'We can't confine our conversations to sex, Harry. That could get a bit boring.'

'The sooner we get bored with each other, the better,' she replied. 'Then I can go back to just being your PA and you can find yourself another dolly-bird to sleep with.'

'I'm sick of sleeping with dolly-birds. I much prefer a woman I can talk to afterwards. Some-one who's on the same wavelength as me. Some-one like you, Harry.'

She rolled her eyes at him. 'In that case, we can talk about work as well as sex.'

Alex's exasperation was interrupted by the waiter arriving with the wine. Alex waved aside the tasting procedure and just asking him to pour, which he did, before placing the bottle in an ice bucket by the table.

'Would you like to order now, sir?' the waiter enquired.

'Come back in a few minutes,' Alex told him.

Harriet picked up her glass and took a sip. Alex did likewise, his mood turning dark as he glared over at her and thought how he much preferred her when she was naked and moaning with de-sire. No sooner had she put her clothes back on than the difficult woman was back, the one who liked rules and checklists, the one who was as intriguing as she was irritating.

* * *

Harriet picked up the menu and pretended to study the courses on offer, but her mind was still on things decidedly sexual. Various erotic images kept popping into her mind, all of them imaginative and wickedly exciting. In the end, she gave up, putting her menu down and picking up her wine glass.

'You order for me, will you?' she asked after a deep swallow of the wine. 'I'm not fussy, especially where seafood is concerned.'

'Right. How about we skip the entree and share a seafood platter? I'm not in the mood for waiting ages between courses.'

Harriet shivered as their eyes met across the table. When he looked at her like that, she wouldn't have minded skipping the whole meal.

'Fine,' she said and took another gulp of wine.

He frowned at her. 'I'd go easy on the alcohol till the food arrives, if I were you. Drinking too much on an empty stomach is never a good idea.'

Harriet's sigh carried exasperation. In truth, the alcohol *was* going straight to her head, but so what? It stopped her worrying about what she was doing and what she was suddenly craving. She was glad when the waiter came back and took their order; glad even when Alex's phone rang, leaving her to sit there and sip her wine in silence while he answered it, her ears pricking up when she heard Alex use the word 'dad'. She'd never heard him talking to family before. Not at work, anyway.

'That's good, Dad,' he was saying. 'No, it's not going to be easy, but it's the only way.'

A short silence, then he added, 'I'm proud of you. Look, I'll talk to you some more tomorrow. I'm out at dinner at the moment. With a very pretty lady.' This with a smile over at her. 'Yes, Dad, I will. Hang in there. Bye for now.'

He hung up, his smile disappearing as he put the phone away.

'My father,' he said unnecessarily, then added, 'He was the family emergency the other day.'

'Oh?' Harriet questioned, not wanting to pry, but naturally curious.

There was instant regret in Alex's eyes. Clearly, he wished he could snatch back those words. But then he shrugged and said bluntly, 'My father's a drunk. He's been living with my sister, Sarah, and giving her grief. Without going into unnecessary detail, I was finally able to get him to go into rehab this week. Hopefully, it will work, but I won't be holding my breath. Still, it gives poor Sarah a decent break.'

Harriet could see that talking about the situation was difficult for him. At the same time, she felt that perhaps he needed to talk about it. Men were their own worst enemy sometimes. They were poor communicators when it came to emotional issues. She wondered if Alex was secretly worried that he might become a drunk, too; that he might have inherited his father's weakness. It would explain why he was careful with alcohol.

'That's sad, Alex. Has your dad always been a heavy drinker?' she asked gently, forcing him to talk about it.

'No. Not at all. It didn't start till after my mother died. She was the love of his life. And the rock in the family. When he lost her from cancer way too early, he couldn't cope. None of us coped all that well. We all adored her, you see. Sarah was devastated. I can't begin to describe how I felt. I found it hard to come to terms with the fact that if she'd been diagnosed earlier, she would probably still be alive.

'Still, none of us kids handled our grief by turning to the bottle. My brother, Roy, eventually took off to the minefields in Western Australia, where he worked seven days a week and made a small fortune for himself. I gather he's married with children now, but we hardly ever hear from him. Sarah became an oncology nurse before getting married and having a family of her own.'

He stopped talking then and lifted his wine glass to his lips, leaving Harriet up in the air as to how *he* had coped with his mother's death. Whilst Harriet could see the danger in continuing with this conversation—her heart had already turned over in sympathy for Alex—she simply could not bear the suspense of not knowing.

'And you, Alex?' she prodded quietly. 'How did *you* cope?'

He shrugged, feeling uncomfortable. He put his glass down and smiled, though the smile didn't reach his eyes. 'I went to Oxford, found two great mates and joined the Bachelor's Club.'

Harriet's eyebrows arched in genuine surprise. 'What on earth is the Bachelor's Club?'

'I thought you didn't want to exchange personal details,' he reminded her.

'That was before.'

'Before what?'

'Before you whetted my curiosity.'

He laughed and the sparkle was back in his eyes. 'Women!' he exclaimed, but on a teasing note.

'Yes, yes, I know. Can't live with them, can't live without them.'

'True. I, for one, could not survive without a woman in my life. And in my bed,' he added, bringing Harriet back to cold, hard realty with a jolt. 'But I have found that the pleasure of a woman's company does come at a price. They invariably want to know way too much about your life, both past and present.'

Harriet stiffened at the injustice of this remark. 'I didn't ask you to tell me about your father's drinking problem, or your mother's death. You volunteered the information.'

He sighed and that bleakness was back in his eyes. 'So I did. Foolish of me. Could you forget I ever mentioned it? It's a rather depressing topic.'

Harriet wondered which one. His father's

drinking problem or his mother's death? She suspected the latter. He must have loved his mother very much. Clearly, his way of coping initially with her death had been to run away from his life here in Australia by studying in England, making friends there and joining this Bachelor's Club.

'I only asked you about the Bachelor's Club, Alex,' she pointed out. 'If you don't want to tell me about it, then fine.'

Their meal arrived at that opportune moment, a simply huge platter full of the most delicious seafood. The tantalising smells wafted up to Harriet's nose, making her mouth water.

'Gosh, that looks good,' she said and the waiter smiled at her. So did Alex.

'Tuck in, then,' he said once the waiter had departed. 'I don't know about you, but I'm suddenly starving.'

They both tucked in, Harriet sampling a little bit of everything. Oysters, lobster, crab, scallops and fish pieces, along with side dishes of French fries and salad. They didn't talk much, and when they did, it was about the food. Alex ordered a second bottle of wine at one stage, though in the end they drank only half of it. He didn't mention the Bachelor's Club again and Harriet decided to let the matter drop. She could read between the lines, anyway. Unlike his sister and brother, Alex had decided that love and marriage were not for him. Maybe he was afraid of the responsibility that marriage entailed. And the emotion. Maybe he was afraid of falling in love. Or maybe he simply wasn't capable of falling in love, his mother's tragic death having killed off that particular part of him. Whatever, Alex obviously liked his life as a bachelor and had no intention of changing. Only a very foolish woman would start thinking—or hoping—that she would be the one to change him.

Harriet liked to think that she wasn't a very foolish woman.

Enjoy what you're doing whilst it lasts, she told herself as she wiped her fingers with her serviette. *Then do what Alex always does—move on!*

CHAPTER THIRTEEN

ALEX GLANCED ACROSS the table and wondered what was going on in Harry's mind. A somewhat defiant light had come into her eyes all of a sudden. Or was it determined? Whatever, he knew that his affair with her was not going to be like any affair he'd ever had before. How could it be? She was different from his usual choice of bed partner. Older, more intelligent and more difficult to control.

Not in bed, though. In a matter of minutes he'd torn down her defences and had her blindly surrendering to his wishes. Clearly, she was a passionate creature whose desire for sex easily matched his. That episode in the shower had been seriously hot. *She* was seriously hot. One night with her would definitely not be enough. One *month* seemed too inadequate as well. Which was a worry. He didn't want to want *any* woman too much. Harriet might start thinking he wanted more from her than just sex. Which he definitely didn't. He liked his life the way it was. He liked being a bachelor with no emotional ties.

It had been a mistake to confide in her the way he had. Big mistake. Like she'd said, confiding in people led to emotional involvement. Alex resolved not to do that again. Right. Time to finish up this meal and take her up to bed, where there would be very little talking. Not on his part, anyway. His tongue would be otherwise occupied. By the time he finished with her tonight, asking him questions about his past life would be the last thing on her mind.

'Do you want dessert?' he asked, only out of sheer politeness.

'Heavens, no,' she replied. 'I've had more calories today than I usually eat in a week.'

'Rubbish. What about coffee?'

'No. I'd rather not sit here any longer, if you don't mind. I can always make us some coffee up in the apartment.'

Alex smiled. 'I do like a girl who knows what she wants.'

'I suppose you think I want you,' she said, her remark surprising him, then annoying him.

Damn, but she was a difficult woman. A great PA, but a pain in the neck as a lover.

'That thought did cross my mind when you kissed me in the shower earlier,' he said in droll tones.

At least he had the satisfaction of seeing a guilty colour enter her cheeks.

'It's been some time since I've had any decent sex,' she said, defiance quickly back in her eyes. 'If I wasn't on the rebound from my relationship with Dwayne, you would never have made it to first base with me.'

The corners of his mouth tilted up into a sardonic smile. 'You honestly believe that?'

Harriet stifled a groan of dismay. What on earth had possessed her to start this type of tit-for-tat conversation? Not only was it dishonest of her, it was potentially humiliating. But, oh…how she'd hated seeing that smug look on his far-too-handsome face, as though it was a foregone conclusion that she would do whatever he wanted. Her pathetic effort to pull his male ego down a peg or two was already in danger of backfiring on her; Alex's bedroom-blue eyes were glittering at her in a wickedly sexy fashion. Clearly, he meant to show her that she was talking rubbish. Which she was. That was the problem.

But she'd be darned if she was going to admit anything. Squaring her shoulders, she found a cool smile from somewhere.

'You do think you're irresistible, don't you?'

'Not at all, but I know what I know. You want me as much as I want you. I'm not afraid to admit it, but you are, for some reason. Silly, really. There's nothing to be gained from your pretending this has something to do with your breaking up with Dwayne. That was just the catalyst which threw us together. You've fallen in lust with me, Harry, and I with you. That's the cold, hard truth of it. Now, do stop putting obstacles in the way of our pleasure. And do stop wasting time. We should be in bed by now, doing what I do very well, and which you have already told me you like a lot. Come…'

When he stood up and reached out his hand towards her, Harriet gave up and gave in.

'You really are an arrogant bastard,' she muttered as she placed her hand in his and let him pull her up onto slightly unsteady feet. Possibly her light-headedness was due to the wine she had drunk, but Harriet doubted it. More likely it was due to the waves of desire that were currently washing through her body. Sweeping up her bag with her free hand, she let Alex steer her from the restaurant, leaving a forlorn-looking waiter in their wake. When she dared to say something, Alex just shrugged and said the charge for the meal would be added to his room account.

Alex didn't say a word to her during their lift ride upwards, or during the short walk along the hallway, the silence only adding to the sexual tension which was gripping Harriet with cruelly frustrating tentacles. Every muscle in her body was tight with need. When she glanced over at Alex, she was taken aback at the tension she glimpsed in *his* face. He hadn't lied to her. He wanted her as much as she wanted him. It was a sinfully seductive thought.

Once they were alone, with the door locked behind them, he turned and yanked her into his arms.

'No more nonsense now,' he ground out after his ravaging kiss reduced them both to heavy breathing. 'You have five minutes to be naked in my bed.'

Alex's lack of sexual inhibition was overwhelming. Yet exciting at the same time.

'Well, what are you waiting for?' he asked, a dry amusement in his voice and eyes.

'You're not just an arrogant bastard,' she threw at him. 'You're a wicked devil as well!' And with that she whirled and flounced off, his laughter following her.

As Alex hurriedly stripped off in the bedroom, he smiled at the memory of the shock that had zoomed into her eyes. Harriet claimed to have been around, but he suspected that her idea of 'been around' was totally different from his. She wasn't even close to being the sophisticated woman of the world she liked to think she was. Not a *femme fatale*, either. But he liked that about her; liked that she could still be shocked.

He couldn't wait to shock her some more.

After a quick trip to the bathroom, Alex collected a new box of condoms from his gym bag, placed it on the bedside table, then climbed, naked, into the bed, his heart thudding with anticipation, his erection bordering on painful. He regretted now not jumping into a cold shower for a couple of minutes, scowling as he conceded he was not going to be able to last all that long the first time. Still, they had all night. He was not a once-a-night man; his sexual stamina was something he'd worked on over the years.

Where *was* that infernal woman? he thought, frustrated as he glared at the still-empty doorway. Five minutes had well and truly gone by now.

Harriet knew she'd passed her five-minute deadline, but she simply could not summon up the courage to walk stark naked into Alex's bedroom. She would have put on the white towelling bathrobe she'd worn earlier, except that it wasn't in her bathroom any more. It was out there somewhere. She hadn't packed a dressing gown, well aware that a five-star resort would provide one. In the end, she grabbed the PJs she'd brought with her and pulled them on. They were hardly the sexiest of outfits, the long pants and long sleeves covering almost every inch of her. And then there were the unfortunate little-girl colours.

The bottom was pink-and-white stripes, the top plain white with little pink love hearts all over it. Emily had bought them for her for her birthday last year.

Thinking of Emily made Harriet groan. Her best friend would have a fit if she knew what she was doing at this moment. Which meant she would never tell her. By the time Emily got back from her holiday, her affair with Alex would probably be over. Taking a couple of deep breaths, Harriet turned and walked from the room with her chin held high. She was shaking inside when she thought of Alex's reaction. He liked to have his orders obeyed...

He was waiting for her on the bed, sitting up with just a sheet over him, a mountain of pillows stuffed behind his head, his magnificent chest bare, his handsome face scowling. But not for long; major amusement rocketed into his eyes as they raked her up and down. He didn't laugh out loud, but he was close.

'I like your idea of naked,' he said, shooting her a heart-stopping smile.

Her stomach flipped right over. 'Sorry. I just couldn't do it.'

'You have no reason to be shy, Harry. You have a very beautiful body.'

Now her *heart* flipped over. *Oh, Harriet, Harriet. Be careful. You don't want to fall in love with this devil. He'll eat you alive.*

She gave him a long, considering look as she walked over to the side of the bed closest to where he was lying. 'I do *not* have a very beautiful body, Alex,' she denied quietly. 'It's nice enough, but not anything special. Please do not feel you have to flatter me. Trust me when I say it's not necessary—I'm a sure thing here.'

Now he laughed. 'That's good to know. When you came in wearing that, I thought you might have changed your mind.'

'Not at all.'

'Then perhaps you could take them off now,' he suggested.

'Is that an order?'

'Not at all,' he replied, cleverly echoing her own words. 'Would you like me to do it for you?'

Yes, she thought with a dizzying rush of desire. But it was imperative she keep some control in all this. Harriet already feared that once she was naked in his bed she might be lost for ever. It was one thing to have a couple of raunchy encounters out of bed, another thing entirely to spend the whole night in his arms.

Scooping in a steadying breath, she slipped off the bottom half of the PJs first, tossing it onto the armchair in the corner, before turning her attention to the top half. Crossing her arms, she lifted it up over her head, hotly aware of the way his eyes were glued to her. When at last she stood naked before him, it took all of her mental and physical strength not to tremble, or to flee. The raw hunger in his gaze was both seductive and terrifying. Had any man ever wanted her like this, and vice versa? Alex had said they'd fallen in lust with each other. Harriet hoped that was all it was.

'And you think you're not anything special,' he growled, shaking his head at her. Throwing back the sheet to reveal his own stunning nakedness, Alex stretched out his hand towards her. 'Now come here, you gorgeous thing, you. I can't wait another second.'

CHAPTER FOURTEEN

HARRIET WOKE IN the same position she'd fallen asleep, lying on her side with Alex's body wrapped around hers like two spoons. His arms were wrapped tightly around her waist, her bottom pressed up against his stomach. She didn't dare move, but whilst her body remained still, her brain was active, reliving their long night of lovemaking.

No, not lovemaking, she amended. *Your long night of sex, dummy. Don't start thinking of it as lovemaking.*

But it had *felt* like lovemaking at the time, she conceded, Alex proving to be a surprisingly tender lover. Imaginative, yes, and totally uninhibited—the things he did with his tongue!—but never had Harriet felt one second of disgust, or even embarrassment. He had a beguiling way about him which bypassed such feelings, caressing her at length between acts of actual intercourse, playing with her body with sometimes shocking intimacy. Yet she had never felt shock, only excitement and pleasure, along with the most amazing orgasms. So many that she had lost count.

Alex had been so right when he'd said she'd fallen in lust with him. She had. Totally.

Her sigh was the sigh of a thoroughly sated woman.

She should have been appalled with herself. But she wasn't. She wasn't even appalled with him. Yet she definitely should have been. If truth be told, Alex was nothing but an arrogant devil with the morals of an alley cat, who thought he could indulge in a strictly sexual affair with his PA, then just shrug her off when he grew bored with her in bed. Which he would. That was the nature of the beast. His admission that he'd always fancied her went some way to excusing his behaviour. But if that was the case, then he should never have hired her, damn him. His lust had become a time bomb waiting to happen.

I never stood a chance, she realised.

Her sigh this time had nothing to do with satisfaction.

'Will you stop all that sighing?' Alex muttered into her hair.

Harriet automatically stiffened, her buttocks tensing when her legs straightened.

He groaned, his hands lifting to cup her breasts as he rolled over onto his back, taking her with him. Panic filled Harriet as the evidence of his erection sent jabs of desire rocketing through her own infatuated flesh. She tried to wriggle away from him, but he held her tight.

'Hand me a condom, beautiful,' he purred into her ear. 'My hands are otherwise occupied.'

Which they were, his palms rubbing over her still-erect nipples, sending unnecessary messages to that part of her which seemed always to be ready for him. Her legs fell apart of their own volition, her belly tightening.

'Haven't you had enough?' Harriet protested, but weakly, her hand already reaching for the condom.

'Not even remotely,' he replied.

Alex had plenty of opportunity to think about that telling reply during the drive back to Sydney.

Harry had refused to put off her Sunday lunch with her friend, despite his doing his best to persuade her over breakfast to stay another night. Whilst she was extremely compliant in bed—*and* in the spa bath this morning—she became a different woman once she was up and dressed, reverting to the difficult one who was not amenable to persuasion.

Alex's decision when he woke this morning to change the rules of their affair looked in danger of failing. When he'd suggested that they meet up at least one night during the week, she had been quick to say no, reminding him that that wasn't what they'd agreed on. She would come to his apartment next Friday night and not before.

Alex couldn't contemplate waiting that long before he made love to her again.

It came to Alex after he'd been driving in a somewhat frustrated silence for over two hours that his PA's hot-as-hell behaviour last night might be worrying her. In his experience, women weren't as pragmatic about sex as men. They read into things. They sometimes invented complications where there weren't any.

Slanting a quick glance her way, he saw that the set of her mouth was tight, her hands gripping her handbag in her lap with unnecessary force. Silly girl. Didn't she know that there was nothing wrong with what they'd done last night? They were consenting adults. Grown-ups. Yet she was sitting there, acting like some guilty schoolgirl or an adulterous wife. Okay, so the suddenness of their affair—and the fieriness of their passion for each other—was on the startling side. But why fight it? Why not just go with the flow and enjoy what they could share till the fire had burned out, after which they could call it quits and she could go back to the life she'd mapped out for herself?

Another reason for her grim mood suddenly crossed Alex's mind. Maybe she was worried that their affair might cost her her job.

He had to say something to reassure her.

'I would never fire you, Harry,' he said. 'If that's what's bothering you.'

Her head turned his way, but she was wearing sunglasses and he couldn't see what was going on in her eyes.

'I know that,' came her rather cool reply.

'Then what *is* bothering you? Are you regretting last night?'

He was taken aback when she laughed. 'Of course,' she said. 'Sleeping with the boss is never a good idea, even if he promises not to fire you when he grows bored with you in bed.'

'I can't see that happening in a hurry,' he muttered. And he meant it. Which was a first for him. Alex had a low boredom threshold at the best of times. He was always looking for new challenges, new goals and, yes, new girlfriends.

Of course, Harry would never be a proper girlfriend. She was going to be his secret mistress, one who would be at his sexual beck and call only at weekends. Stupid rule, that. He had been an idiot ever to suggest such a masochistic arrangement.

'I have no illusions,' came her firm pronouncement, 'about how this affair of ours will end.'

Maybe it will never end, Harry, came the unexpected thought. *Maybe I will keep you as my secret mistress for ever.*

It was a truly wicked thought. But a hell of an appealing one. People said you could never have your cake and eat it, too. But maybe he could. At least for a while. There was no hurry for her to get married, surely? She was only twenty-nine. Women got married later these days. And had children later. He would have to let her go eventually, he supposed. But till then he aimed to make her his. *Without* all these silly rules.

For the first time during this exasperating drive, Alex's black mood lifted. Knowing what you wanted in life was always a good thing, he accepted. And he wanted Harriet. Not just for a few weeks. For much, *much* longer than that.

'It's never a wise thing to think about endings, Harry,' he said, adopting his best salesman voice. 'Far better to live in the moment. The only assurance we have in life is the here and now. You like having sex with me, don't you?'

She sighed. 'You know I do.'

'Then stop stressing and just enjoy. We could be dead tomorrow.'

When he glanced over at her, he saw that she was frowning.

'I can't think like that,' she said. 'I have to plan. *You* plan. You plan all the time. So stop giving me this "live in the moment" nonsense, Alex. If you think you can persuade me to change my mind where the rules of our affair are concerned, then you can think again.'

Alex gritted his teeth. Lord, but she would try the patience of a saint. And he was no saint. He was, however, a man who rose to a challenge.

Relaxing the clenched muscles in his jaw took an effort, but he managed before shooting her a warmly amused smile. 'Can't blame a man for trying, Harry. Last night was so fabulous that I find it unbearable to wait another week to sample some more of your bewitching charms.'

'*You* were the one who claimed sex was better if you wait.'

He smiled with amusement at the cleverness of her mind. And the sharpness of her wit. 'Yes, well, there's waiting and waiting. I was talking about a few hours on that occasion, not a whole week. I would imagine that by Friday night I'll be ready to explode.'

'Too much information,' she threw at him.

He laughed, then she laughed, breaking the tension that had been building since they'd set off.

'That's better,' he said.

'Better?' she echoed.

'I wasn't looking forward to sitting next to Miss Grumpy all the way back to Sydney.'

'I wasn't grumpy. I was just…thinking.'

'Thinking is almost as bad as planning. Or so Jeremy tells me. He doesn't believe in either.'

'Your best friend, Jeremy? The rake from London?'

'The one and the same.'

'He sounds very shallow.'

'Oh, he is. He admits it. But he's also intelligent and charming and the most wonderful friend I've ever had. Outside of Sergio, that is.'

'I presume it's Sergio, then, who's getting married.'

'Yes, the poor devil.'

'Why do you say it like that? What have you got against marriage?'

'Don't misunderstand me. I have nothing against marriage. It's the woman he's marrying that worries me.'

'What's wrong with her?'

For a split second, Alex hesitated. But then he told her. All about Sergio and Bella, detailing their past history and their current romance. She was taken aback at the identity of the bride-to-be, of course. Bella was very well known in Australia. But so was her reputation with men.

'I can understand why you're worried,' she said.

'Thank God someone agrees with me. Jeremy has some doubts, but he believes that they're genuinely in love.'

'It does happen, you know. People do fall in love.'

'Not that quickly. It's nothing but lust. Which is not a recipe for marital happiness. You need to be best friends as well as lovers. Soul mates, for want of a better word.'

'In an idealistic world, perhaps. Life is not always quite so accommodating.'

'I suppose so. I have an awful feeling that Sergio loves Bella, but that she's only in it for the money. Being a billionaire is not always an advantage when it comes to finding true love.'

'Well, you don't have to worry about that, Alex. You're not interested in finding true love.'

'You are absolutely correct. That kind of love is not for me.'

Harriet wondered just *why* Alex was so against falling in love. He must have been badly hurt at one stage to feel so strongly about it. Before she could come to any conclusion, he turned and smiled at her.

'The turn-off for Taree is coming up. What say we get off the freeway and go have some lunch?'

CHAPTER FIFTEEN

IT WAS AFTER five before Alex pulled up outside her flat. Harriet was annoyed with herself when she asked him if he'd like to come up for a cup of coffee. What had happened to her resolve to keep some control over their affair and her own silly self? To invite him into her home was a foolish move. But it was done now.

Of course, he said yes, that big, bad wolf smile on his face.

At least he carried her bag up the stairs for her, her flat being on the second floor of the rather ancient red-brick building. There were eight units in all, hers at the front of the building facing east, though not with an ocean view, being a couple of streets back from the beach.

'Nice place you've got here, Harry,' Alex said even before she'd shown him inside. He knew she owned it. She'd said so when he'd interviewed her.

'I like it,' she replied, fishing out her key and opening the front door.

'*Very* nice,' he said once he went inside and glanced around.

His compliment pleased her, Harriet being on the house-proud side, something she'd learned from her mother, who had instilled in her daughter good habits when it came to keeping her home clean and tidy. Harriet's good taste in furniture and furnishings, however, was something she'd learned for herself after coming to Sydney. Selling expensive real estate did give one a yearning for having nice things around.

Her two-bedroomed flat wasn't overly large, but by painting all the walls and ceilings white, and not overfurnishing the rooms, she'd achieved the effect of making it look larger than it was. Both the kitchen and bathrooms were white, but that was not her doing. They'd been renovated shortly before she'd bought the place.

'Could you point me to the bathroom, Harry?' Alex asked.

She did, reminding him that the light in there wasn't working due to her poor DIY skills.

'Give me a bulb, then,' Alex said. 'I'll fix it while I'm here. You go make the coffee.'

He joined her in the kitchen a couple of minutes later. 'All fixed,' he said.

'Thank you,' she said. 'I didn't realise you would be such a good handyman.'

He laughed. Not a happy laugh. More a dry one. 'When you grow up living in government housing, you learn to do all minor repairs yourself. If there was one thing Dad did teach me growing up, it was how to change light bulbs and tap washers. I can also fix leaking toilets and blocked drains. So, if your kitchen sink ever gets blocked up...' he added, smiling wryly.

'I will call a plumber,' Harriet finished for him, at the same time wondering if Alex had called his dad today like he promised last night. She hadn't heard him do so. Still, it really wasn't her business to remind him. It wasn't like they were at work, when she often reminded him to do things. He could be forgetful at times. Oh, Lord, maybe she *should* say something...

'You're frowning,' he said. 'On top of that, you've stopped making the coffee. What gives?'

Harriet turned to look at him. 'I'm worried that

you might have forgotten to ring your dad. You promised him last night that you would call him today.'

Alex shook his head at her. 'I should never have told you about him.'

'Well, you *did*,' she replied, feeling quite angry with his attitude. 'And I'm glad you did. Now at least I know that you're human, with personal problems like the rest of us.'

His eyebrows lifted. 'Wow, Harry, you have quite a temper on you, don't you? Something you've managed to keep hidden from me all these months.'

'A PA doesn't lose her temper with her boss. But a secret mistress is another thing entirely. Tamper with a woman's emotions and you have to pay the price.'

'I don't want to tamper with your emotions. Just your body.'

'Same thing, Alex. I'm a woman. Our bodies and our emotions are linked. Unlike men. It always amazes me how some men can compartmentalise their lives. Work over here and women over there. In the past, you've cleverly chosen to sleep with empty-headed young things who haven't given you any trouble. Let me warn you in advance, Alex, that I might give you trouble.'

His eyes narrowed on her. 'Are you warning me that you might fall in love with me?'

'I certainly hope not,' she said quite truthfully. 'But don't expect me to be entirely happy with this…relationship. Yes, I love having sex with you, and yes, I love working for you. But I'm going to find it increasingly hard to separate the two. Please appreciate that I might have to quit in the end.'

'Quit work or quit me?'

'Both.'

'I won't let you.'

A shiver of alarm ran down her spine at the sheer arrogance of him.

'You won't have any choice in the matter.'

'We'll see about that,' he ground out. 'Forget the coffee. I'm going home. But first a little taste of what you can expect next Friday night.'

Five minutes later, he was gone, leaving Harriet reeling with shock. She sagged back against the kitchen counter, her legs weak with desire. What a cruel devil he was, kissing her like that, then touching her like that, bringing her to the brink of release, then just abandoning her, his eyes glittering with a chilling resolve when his head finally lifted.

The week that stretched ahead of her would be unbearable. But of course Alex wanted it to be. That was why he'd just done what he'd done.

I should never have challenged him like that, Harriet conceded as she levered herself away from the kitchen counter, pulled her bra back into place, then did up her jeans. She'd known from the start that she was way out of her league, tangling with someone like Alex.

Try as she might, however, Harriet could not regret going to bed with him. How could she regret something which had brought her so much pleasure? Alex excited her as no man had ever excited her. He was a fabulous lover, with a way about him that was both seductive and oddly romantic. The compliments he'd made about her body last night were so sweet. Harriet knew she wouldn't be the one to call it quits. But *he* would one day, and this inevitability would happen sooner rather than later if she didn't lighten up a bit. She really had to stop acting the way she had earlier today. And just now. She had to start doing what Alex suggested. Live for the moment. Concentrate on just having fun!

It came to Harriet that she'd never been a 'just have fun' girl. She'd always been so serious. But it wasn't too late, surely? She could do fun, couldn't she? Not every relationship had to be about finding Mr Right. After the fiasco with Dwayne, that could definitely wait for a while. As for that stupid checklist of hers, that was definitely going to be thrown out the window.

Satisfied with her new resolve, Harriet made her way back into the living room, where Alex had left her bag. She had just picked it up when her phone rang. Dropping the bag, she walked over to where she'd placed her handbag on the dining table, retrieved her phone, then groaned. It was Emily. Oh, Lord. She had a sinking feeling that Emily might have found out about Dwayne.

'Hi, Em,' she said with false brightness. 'How's it going with the holiday?'

'Don't you say hi to me like that, Harriet Mc-Kenna. Why didn't you ring and tell me that you've broken up with Dwayne? All those text messages about work and not a single word about what's really important.'

Harriet scooped in a deep breath, then let it out slowly before answering.

'Why do you think?' she finally asked. 'I knew you wouldn't be on my side and I wasn't in the mood for a lecture.'

'Don't be silly. Of course I'm on your side. You're my best friend. Dwayne doesn't mean a thing to me. Okay, so I thought you and he were a good match, but it's what *you* think that really counts. Obviously, you decided he wasn't the right man for you.'

A huge lump had filled Harriet's throat at this unexpected show of support from Emily. She'd been so sure that she would be critical.

'No, he wasn't,' she choked out. 'I…I…' Her voice cut out as her whole chest filled with emotion, tears threatening. Silly, really, given she'd already realised she hadn't loved Dwayne.

'Oh, Harriet. Hon,' Emily said gently. 'I didn't mean to upset you.'

Harriet gulped, then cleared her throat. 'I thought you'd be mad at me.'

'Never. I just worry about you, that's all. I want you to be happy.'

'I want to be happy, too.'

'Then perhaps you should stop looking for Mr Perfect to marry and just have fun for a while,' Emily suggested. 'You're still young, Harriet. Plenty of time for you to get married yet.'

'You're so right, Em. I've been thinking exactly the same thing.'

CHAPTER SIXTEEN

'GOT ANYTHING SPECIAL planned for this week-end?' Audrey asked Harriet.

Friday night had finally arrived and the two women were sharing a bottle of white wine at the nearby hotel where the staff of Ark Properties gathered for drinks every Friday night after work. Audrey and Harriet were sitting at a quiet table in a dark corner, whilst the boys were gathered at the bar drinking beer and watching the Friday night football game. Alex was noticeably absent, as he'd been from the office most of the week, finding any and every excuse to go out—minus his PA—from business lunches to doing site-checks of all their current building projects. He'd claimed he had to have everything on track before leaving for Milan the following week, though Harriet suspected he just didn't want to be around her lest he be tempted to go back on his word.

When she'd arrived at work last Monday morning, a bagel already in hand, she'd made Alex coffee and taken both into his office, where she'd apologised for being so uptight the other night. She'd promised to lighten up in future, adding that she didn't want to live her life according to rules, and it would be all right with her if he wanted to see her before Friday night. He'd stared at her for a long moment, then told her that he would prefer to wait till Friday as they'd originally agreed upon. Although surprised and a little hurt, the new live-for-the-moment, just-have-fun Harriet simply smiled and said fine. Whatever.

But it had been a long, long week.

'No, nothing special,' Harriet told Audrey, hoping the lie didn't show in her eyes. 'I might try to catch up on housework. I usually give the flat a thorough clean on a Saturday, but I was away last Saturday.'

'That's right. You were up north with Alex. How did that go, by the way?'

Harriet shrugged. 'Okay. I think Alex was annoyed that the rain had delayed things so much. No way is that golf course going to be open by Christmas.'

'It's supposed to rain all next week, too,' Audrey said. 'Not just here in Sydney, but all the way up the coast.'

Harriet groaned. 'He's not going to be too thrilled with that.'

'Nothing you can do about the weather,' Audrey said. 'Where did you stay?'

'Oh, some place near Coffs Harbour. Quite nice, really. You know Alex. He wouldn't stay at a dump.'

'Why should he? I mean, he's seriously rich. And seriously sexy. I would watch yourself with him, if I were you.'

'What do you mean?'

'You know what I mean. Now that Dwayne's out of the picture…' Audrey shrugged, then took another sip of her wine.

No way did Harriet want any of the staff ever to know about her affair with Alex. Though they might twig after she resigned. But it wouldn't matter then.

'He's not really my type,' Harriet said. 'But I know what you mean. He *is* handsome, but personally I don't like arrogant men.'

Audrey frowned at her over the rim of her glass. 'I thought you liked Alex.'

'Well, yes, I do. And to be fair, he's not all that arrogant. But he can be annoying at times.'

'Yes, I can see that. Rich bachelors like him are not used to considering other people's feelings. They don't mean to be selfish or self-centred, but they are.'

'You've got it in one,' Harriet stated, thinking that was Alex's biggest flaw. His selfishness. At the same time, however, he could be kind, generous and even rather sweet. She would never forget what he'd done for Romany.

But he should never have pursued *her*. That had not been kind, or sweet. It had been seriously selfish. He could have slept with just about any other woman in Sydney, but he had to pick her.

Such thinking suddenly annoyed Harriet, who'd determined to put aside the critical habits of her old, serious self and embrace a more easy-going attitude to life and men. So, instead of criticising Alex in her head, she focused on his good points. He gave oodles of money to charity, was a caring son and a fabulous lover. This last fact reminded her that in less than two hours she'd be in his arms again, being made love to in ways she'd only ever dreamt about. The anticipation of what was in store for her tonight had her shifting restlessly in her seat. Her phone suddenly ringing startled her, the identity of the caller startling her as well.

'Hi there,' she answered, careful not to say Alex's name.

'I presume you're still at the pub,' he ground out.

'Yes, I am.'

'Don't say my name,' he warned her sharply.

'I won't. What's up?' If he was calling to tell her not to come, she would just die.

'Is there any chance you can make it before nine?' he asked.

Nine was the time he'd designated before he'd left the office that morning, giving her a key-card at the same time so that she could access the building and the private lift to the penthouse.

'I'm going insane here,' he added thickly.

The passion and the urgency in his voice was both flattering and arousing. Not that Harriet needed arousing. She was already burning for him.

'Me, too,' she said quietly.

'Have you eaten?'

'Not yet.'

'Then don't. I've organised something for later. Can you come straight away?'

'I should be able to. I'll catch a taxi and meet you there ASAP. Bye.'

Putting her phone away, she rose and threw Audrey an apologetic smile. 'Sorry to abandon you so early, but I'm needed.'

'Oh?'

'A married girlfriend of mine has the chance of a rare night out while her husband minds the baby, so we're off to a movie together.'

'What are you going to see?'

'Have no idea. Have to go. See you on Monday.' And she bolted before Audrey could ask her any more awkward questions.

The hotel was within walking distance of the taxi rank down at the quay. Harriet didn't have to wait too long before she was climbing into the back seat and giving the driver Alex's address. But it was Friday night, of course, with Friday night traffic. Her level of frustration rose when it took ten minutes to go three blocks. She sent

Alex a text message explaining she was on her way but the traffic was heavy.

No sweat, came his reply. I'll meet you downstairs.

He was standing on the pavement by the time she climbed out of the taxi, dressed in a black tracksuit with a white T-shirt underneath and white trainers. Harriet still had on the tailored black suit and white silk blouse that she'd worn to work, actually having planned to go home before coming here tonight to shower and change into something more feminine. She'd also planned to put on the new sexy black underwear that she'd bought this week.

During the ride in the taxi, she'd regretted not having the opportunity to dolly herself up for Alex, but at the sight of him she no longer cared. The way he was looking at her made her not care about anything but being here with him.

He didn't say a word, just took her arm and urged her through the revolving glass doors inside the foyer, which was modern and spacious with a large reception desk, behind which sat two burly security guards studying computer screens. They didn't even look up as Alex steered her across the vast expanse of marble tiled floor to an alcove which housed the lifts. There were four in all, Alex choosing the one marked for private use only. The doors opened immediately, Alex ushering her into the lavishly appointed lift that had lots of brass and glass, along with far too much lighting. Harriet could see her reflection everywhere, forcing her to note her flushed face and her over-bright eyes.

'How long have you lived here?' she asked him in an effort to break the tension which was almost killing her. If her heart beat any faster, she was sure it would explode.

Alex pressed the button which had the lift doors closing with barely a sound before he turned and answered her.

'About three years. I bought it off-plan five years ago before it was even built and before the market went crazy. God, but it's been a long week. I have to kiss you, Harry. I simply can't wait.' He pulled her into his arms and kissed her right there in the lift. Even when it reached its destination, and the doors slid quietly open, the kissing didn't stop. By then he'd rammed her up against the mirrored back wall, the coldness of the glass seeping through her jacket. Not that she cared. She was way too hot to care about such a small discomfort. By then her handbag had fallen from numb fingers and her arms were wrapped tightly around his neck. His hands were much busier, hitching up her skirt, pushing aside her panties.

She moaned when his fingers found their target. God, she was close to coming. And she didn't care. She *needed* to come. *Yes, yes, just keep doing that*; all her muscles tensed in anticipation of release from the madness which was possessing her.

His taking his hand away brought a groan of despair, her eyes flying open when his head lifted. His expression was wry and knowing.

'Sorry, but I had to stop,' he said.

She just stared at him, her heartbeat still haywire. 'You're cruel,' she said shakily.

'Sometimes you have to be cruel to be kind. I didn't have a condom with me and I was close to losing control. For some reason kissing you does that to me,' he said and reached out to run a single fingertip over her still-burning mouth.

'I suspect you have some secret aphrodisiac in this red lipstick you always wear.'

She couldn't speak, all her attention on that tantalising fingertip.

His eyes darkened on her, aware no doubt of the extent of her desire.

'Come,' he said, this time taking her arm more gently.

Alex guided her across a wide entrance hall and into a huge living room which was beautifully appointed, filled with glass and white leather furniture which shouted money. The floors were all grey marble tiles, but the rugs were thick, soft and more colourful. The artwork on the walls were probably originals, not the framed prints which graced her own flat.

'This way,' he said, leading her past a semi-circular shaped alcove in which sat a circular glass dining table beautifully set for two, with elegant silver placemats and tall candles just waiting to be lit.

'That's for dinner later,' he told her, perhaps noting the direction of her eyes.

'It looks lovely.' She hadn't expected anything so romantic.

'I've ordered a meal to be delivered at ten from a local restaurant. And there's two bottles of chilled white wine waiting for you in the fridge.'

'You've thought of everything,' she said, taken aback by his thoughtful attention to detail.

'I try to please. I would have been showered and properly attired if my passion for you hadn't got the better of me. But while I was waiting for you to arrive, I realised I could kill two birds with one stone.'

'Sorry. I'm not following you.'

'You will. This way…'

He took her down a tiled hallway and into the master bedroom, which was large, spacious and thankfully nothing like a playboy's bedroom, other than the fact that the bed was king-sized. The floor was covered in a lush cream carpet, the furniture made in a dark wood, the furnishings in various shades of cream and brown. She loved the brass-based bedside lamps with their stylish cream shades and the gorgeous tapestry which hung above the bedhead. It was a park scene—Parisian, since it had the Eiffel Tower in the background. The colours were glorious.

'I love that tapestry,' she said as he led her past it.

'It's a recent purchase. An investment, really. I don't put my money in stock and shares. I prefer property. And art.'

Harriet couldn't afford to invest in art. But at least she did have her flat, which had already doubled in value since she'd bought it.

'In here,' he directed and guided her into an *en suite* bathroom which had to be seen to be believed. It was larger than her bedroom with a modern toilet and bidet, a sunken spa bath, a double vanity and a shower stall built for two. Or possibly three. But it wasn't any of those things which made her gasp. It was the candles which were dotted around the bath, all lit and giving out the most incredible vanilla fragrance.

'Did you do this for me?' she asked, amazed and touched.

His smile was warm, soft and faintly apologetic. 'I wanted to make it up to you for being a bit of a bastard last Monday. All I can say in my defence is that I knew I wouldn't be able to get all the work done that I needed to do before I went away if I started meeting up with you. And making love to you. And not getting any sleep. As it was, I didn't sleep all that well anyway, despite working my butt off in the gym every evening. All I could think about was you, Harry.'

'Oh...' she said, in danger of melting into a puddle. 'I...I didn't sleep very well, either.'

His smile was slow, sexy and incredibly arousing. 'That's nice to know,' he said as he turned on the bath taps, adjusted the temperature, then tipped in what looked like bubble bath. 'Can you wait a bit longer?' he asked her as he turned back to face her.

'What? Yes. No. Yes, I...I suppose so.'

'Good. Now I'm going to take off all your clothes.'

'What?'

'Don't think about it. Just let me do it.'

She didn't think about it, and she let him do it, dazed by the feeling of blissful helplessness which took possession of her as he slowly removed each item of clothing. First came her jacket, which he folded and placed on the vanity counter top. Her blouse followed, then her bra.

How weird it felt to be standing before Alex, naked to her waist. Weird, yet wickedly exciting.

Her skirt came next, then her shoes, leaving her with nothing on but a black satin thong and a pair of lace-topped stay-up stockings.

Once she was naked, he took a step back and just looked at her.

'That's how I've been picturing you all week,' he said thickly, his eyes raking over her.

She'd done a lot of picturing of her own, her many erotic fantasies underlining just how much in lust with Alex she was. Lord, if he didn't make love to her soon, she was going to faint with desire. Her head was spinning, whilst the rest of her was on fire.

'Aren't you going to get undressed?' she asked him shakily.

'Of course. Do you want to watch?'

Oh, Lord, she was seriously out of her depth here.

He didn't strip slowly, but he didn't hurry, either. Once naked, he turned off the taps, then extracted a condom from a nearby drawer, ripping it open with his teeth before drawing it on with practised swiftness. She tried not to stare, but he was just so big and hard and ready. She wanted him inside her right now.

'I...I don't think I can wait much longer,' she told him shakily.

He smiled a wry smile. 'Me neither, beautiful.'

Taking her shoulders, he turned her to face the vanity mirror. Without his saying a word, she knew what he wanted her to do. She reached out to grip the edges of the marble bench top, moved her legs apart, then bent forward, dropping her head so that she couldn't see the wantonness in her eyes. She gasped when he stroked down the curve of her spine, caressing her bottom before taking a firm hold of her hips and doing what she was desperate for him to do.

Oh, God, she thought as her head spun and her body rocketed to a release that saw her crying out like some wild, wounded animal. He came soon after her, pulling her upright as his flesh shuddered within hers. When their eyes finally met in the mirror, his smile stunned her. For it was soft and sweet, making her heart lurch in a way that might have worried her at any other time. But her mind was on other things at that moment.

'I like the new you, Harry,' he said, a wicked twinkle in his eye. 'Now, let's go get in that bath.'

CHAPTER SEVENTEEN

I DON'T WANT her to go, Alex thought as he reluctantly followed Harry to the lift doors.

He'd never enjoyed a weekend so much in years. Never enjoyed a woman so much in years. It wasn't just the sex part—though that was fabulous—it was her company, her conversation, her intelligence. Alex hadn't realised till that weekend how much he craved being with a woman as smart as she was. And Harriet was smart. Perhaps not academically. She didn't have degrees to her name. But she had smarts of a different kind. She was quite well-read, too, he'd found out. Plus she was never at a loss for words. Or opinions. They hadn't spent the whole weekend having sex, though Friday night had been full on. Understandable, given they'd both been somewhat frustrated at the time.

After a long sleep-in on the Saturday, he'd driven her back to her place so that she could get a change of clothes. When he then suggested they drive out somewhere for lunch, she hadn't objected, so he'd headed west toward the Blue Mountains, showing her the parcels of land he'd bought near the proposed new airport at Badgery's Creek on the way. Her praise over his plan to build affordable housing for the people who would one day work at the airport had pleased him no end. He rarely told anyone about his charitable efforts, most people not being interested. But Harry had seemed genuinely impressed.

After lunch at a trendy café in Katoomba, they'd visited the Three Sisters, where Harry had taken heaps of photos of the iconic mountaintops, insisting he be in most of the shots. It had been a fun day. By the time they'd arrived back at his apartment, however, he'd been more than ready to take her to bed. He'd ordered Chinese that night and they'd eaten it whilst they watched a movie, their naked bodies wrapped in a mohair rug he kept on the sofa. Then it had been back to bed, where they'd stayed on and off for the whole of Sunday, only rising to shower and eat.

When Harry had said around five that she really had to go home, he'd tried to change her mind with some more lovemaking. But it had worked only temporarily. By five-thirty she was adamant that it was time for her to go. Sighing, he said he would drive her home. But he still hated the thought of her going. When the temptation arose to ask her to move in with him, he was totally taken aback. That was not what he wanted in life. Besides, he was pretty sure that Harry would say no. She just wanted to have fun with him, not live with him. Though he didn't abandon the idea altogether...

'Come with me,' he said when they stopped at a set of lights during the drive to her place. 'To Italy.'

Harriet's head whipped round, his offer clearly having thrown her. 'I can't do that,' she said at last. 'People at work will talk.'

'They don't have to know. I'll go into the office on Monday and say you've come down with a bad case of flu. I'll say I've given you the week off.'

He could see that she was tempted. Seriously tempted.

'I don't know, Alex,' she said slowly. 'I don't think it's a good idea.'

'Well, I do. You can come to the wedding with

me, then afterwards I'll take you to Venice for a couple of days.'

'Venice,' she repeated, her eyes going all misty. 'I've always wanted to go to Venice.'

The lights went green and he drove on. 'Then let me take you there,' he said.

She shook her head at him. 'You are a wicked man, do you know that?'

'It has been said of me before. But I don't think it's wicked to offer to take you to Italy with me. You'll love Lake Como.'

'I dare say I will. I've heard it's very beautiful. But I won't go to the wedding with you. I wouldn't be comfortable doing that. They are *your* friends, Alex, not mine.'

Alex knew when he'd pushed things as far as he could.

'Very well. I'll book you into a nearby hotel on the lake whilst I'm doing my best man act. You can do a few touristy things by yourself that day. Then, after the wedding, I'll join you and we'll go to Venice together.'

'Won't that take longer than a week?'

He shrugged. 'Not much longer. Look, as things stand I won't be back by next weekend. I don't know about you, but I've enjoyed this weekend more than even I envisaged. I love your company, Harry, in bed *and* out. Come with me. Please...'

Harriet didn't speak again for a full minute. 'I should say no,' she said. But there was a smile in her voice.

He grinned. 'Possibly. But you're not going to. You're going to fly first class with me to Italy.'

'No,' she replied with a firmness which shocked him. 'I'm not.'

Before he could give vent to his frustration, she added, '*You* can fly first class, but *I'll* be in economy. I wouldn't feel comfortable having you pay that much money for my flight.'

'But I can afford it,' he told her.

'I don't care what you can afford. I will not be bought, Alex. I'm not that kind of girl.'

'Would you compromise by going business class?'

She heaved a resigned sigh. 'I suppose that would be all right. But I will be paying for my own ticket. I also want to pay half of all our hotel expenses. And before you object, I assure you, *I* can afford it. I'll just use the money I saved up for my wedding. I only lost the deposit on the reception venue when I broke up with Dwayne, so I have plenty left.'

Alex frowned. 'But surely your parents were going to pay for your wedding?'

Her laugh sounded bitter. 'My parents and I are estranged,' she told him. 'They wouldn't have come to my wedding even if I'd invited them. Which I had no intention of doing.'

Shock at this statement was quickly followed by curiosity.

'What on earth happened between you?'

'My father happened, that's what,' she stated with a bitterness which stunned him.

Alex recalled her telling him something at her interview about her father losing his job when she'd been a teenager, which was why she'd had to go out to work instead of studying. He'd been a miner up in the Singleton area. But that was all he knew about her family.

'He was a pig,' Harriet bit out. 'A male chauvinist pig.'

Whoa, Alex thought. They were pretty heavy words.

'What did he do?' Alex asked.

'What didn't he do?' she threw at him. 'First,

he thought women were only put on this earth to wait on him hand and foot. Mum and I were treated like servants. Never with love or caring. My brothers were spoiled rotten, whilst I got nothing. He bought them everything they wanted, whereas I was given only the barest essentials. I lived in second-hand uniforms and clothes. If it hadn't been for gifts from relatives, I would never have had anything new.'

Alex could hardly believe what he was hearing. He'd been critical of his father at times, but he was still a loving parent. What little money he'd earned, he'd given to his children.

'I lied when I told you that Dad had lost his job,' Harriet went on. 'He never did. He always earned a good salary. But Mum and I never saw any of it. So, once I was old enough to get a job or three, I did so.' A small, very bitter smile curved her mouth. 'Naturally, Dad was furious when I refused to hand over any of my salaries.'

'He didn't hit you, did he?' Alex despised men who hit women.

'No. He wasn't a physically violent man, just verbally and emotionally abusive. I hated him.'

'Understandable. So I'm presuming you didn't

have your parents' approval when you came to Sydney to pursue a career in real estate?'

'They had absolutely no idea of my plans. But I always knew what I was going to do. First, I saved up for a car. Not a new car, of course. But not bad, either. I also secretly went to college at night, doing an advanced computer course as well as getting my real-estate licence. Then, as soon as I turned twenty, I left home and drove the two hundred kilometres to Sydney.'

'That was brave of you,' he said, admiring her enormously.

'I didn't see it that way. I just knew I had to leave home and make a life for myself. I had enough money saved to survive for a few weeks till I got a job. And I booked into a backpackers' lodge till then as it was relatively cheap.'

'Did you tell your parents you were going or did you just up and leave?'

'Mum knew I was going, but Dad was at work when I left. I did ring home to tell Mum I'd arrived safely, but Dad answered and promptly disowned me, saying I was ungrateful and that he didn't want to set eyes on me ever again.'

'You're right. He is a pig. I hope you told him where to go.'

'I did indeed. In no uncertain terms. Then when I asked to speak to my mother, he hung up. I did ring again the next day when I knew he'd be at work, but Mum also hung up on me.'

Her sad sigh was very telling. 'Clearly, she'd been ordered not to talk to me, and she was too scared to defy him. I'd hoped I might be able to persuade her to leave him, but I soon saw that was never going to happen. I knew from that moment on that I was on my own. My life would be what *I* made it. No one was going to help me.'

Alex was beginning to understand exactly where that checklist had come from. It went a long way back.

'Well, you've done a very good job,' he complimented her. 'I was seriously impressed when I read your résumé, working your way up from being a receptionist to getting a job in sales. Not for any old company, either. For one of Sydney's top realtors. Frankly, I was a bit surprised when you applied for the job as my PA. You probably could have made more money staying in sales.'

'Life isn't all about money, Alex.'

'It's still nice to have it,' he replied.

'True. Right, we're nearly there. I suggest you just let me off outside my place, Alex. There'll be no parking in my street on a Sunday afternoon.'

She was right. There wasn't. 'Are you absolutely sure you have to go home?' he tried one last time. 'I could always turn around and take you back to my place for the night.'

'Alex, just stop it,' she said firmly. 'If I'm going to Italy with you on Tuesday, I have lots of things to do.'

'Give me a kiss before you go.'

She laughed. 'Good try, Alex.' And she was out of the car like a shot, leaning in to grab her overnight bag before waving and running inside.

Alex just sat there for a long moment, then drove slowly back to his place, feeling more alone than he ever had in his life before. Once there, he wandered around like a lost sheep for a while till in desperation he rang Sergio and talked for a good twenty minutes, unlike his previous congratulatory call, which had been rather brief. By the time he hung up, Alex saw what Jeremy meant about their friend being genuinely in love with Bella. He was utterly obsessed with the woman, unable to form a sentence without her name being in it. Alex hoped like hell that Sergio's love was returned. Falling that deeply in love could be dangerous enough. Even worse if it was one-sided.

Seeking more reassurance on the matter, he rang Jeremy, who clearly didn't appreciate being woken on a Sunday morning before noon.

'Alex,' he growled. 'Do you know what time it is?'

'I guess that depends on where you are. London or Lake Como?'

'Neither. I'm in Paris.'

'What are you doing in Paris?'

'What do you think I'm doing in Paris? Go back to sleep, *mon amie*,' he murmured to whoever was in bed beside him. 'So what drama is unfolding in your life that you feel you have to call me at this ungodly hour? It had better be life threatening, or you're a dead man.'

'No drama on my front,' he said, though his mind flew to a certain brunette who was definitely giving him grief. 'I've just been talking to Sergio. Hell, Jeremy, the poor man is seriously infatuated, isn't he?'

'Seriously in love, more like it. And Bella is, too, so you can stop worrying about their marriage. I'm beginning to think that it just might work.'

'How can you be sure? About *her* feelings, that is?'

'I can just tell. The way they look at each other and speak about each other. It's positively sickening. If I ever act like that around a woman, I want you to shoot me.'

Alex laughed. 'I don't have a gun.'

'I'll give you one. We have several in the gun room at the family's country estate.'

'Remind me not to go there with you any more.'

'Don't be ridiculous, you love it there. What say we pop down together for a few days after the wedding? It's lovely in Cornwall in the summer.'

At any other time, he would have said yes. But as much as he loved Jeremy's excellent company, it could not compare with being in Venice with Harriet. Not that he could say that.

'Sorry. No can do. I have to get back here ASAP. I'm up to my ears in work.'

Jeremy sighed. 'Truly, Alex, someone is going

to have to take you in hand one day and teach you how to relax.'

Alex smiled as he thought about where Harry's hand had been earlier today. Not that he'd felt in any way relaxed at the time.

'Well, if anyone could teach me how to relax, it would be you,' he said. 'If R and R was a sport, you'd win the gold medal every four years.'

Jeremy chuckled. 'I'll take that as a compliment. But honestly, dear friend, all work and no play makes Alex a dull boy.'

'In that case, you'll be pleased to know I've been playing all weekend.' As soon as the bragging words were out of his mouth, he regretted them.

'*Really?* Do tell.'

'Sorry, mate, I'm not a kiss-and-tell kind of guy.'

'So, how old is this latest bimbo of yours?'

'I'll have you know she's in her late twenties. And no bimbo.'

'I'm impressed. What does she do for a crust?'

Alex had to think quickly. He could hardly say she was his PA. 'She's in real estate,' he said.

'Even better. Nothing worse than dating someone with very little between her ears.'

Alex had noticed over the years that Jeremy preferred intelligent girls, provided they were beautiful as well as brainy.

'So, who did you bring to Paris?' Alex asked.

'No one. Marlee lives in Paris. She's an editor. I'm going to put her in charge of my French office.'

'Combining business and pleasure is never a good idea,' Alex said with considerable irony.

'What rubbish. I've had some of my best sex by doing just that. Look, something's just come up. So I should go. Text me the details of your flight and I'll meet you at Milan airport. *Au revoir.*'

Alex had no time to open his mouth before Jeremy hung up. Smiling wryly over what it was that had come up, Alex put down his phone, then made his way out to the kitchen, where he poured himself a large glass of Scotch, added a few ice cubes, then returned to the living room, sipping slowly. Calling his two best friends hadn't helped all that much. He still missed Harriet and she'd been gone only an hour or so. The thought that he might be falling in love with her started worrying him. He didn't want to fall for her any more than she wanted to fall for him. They had different goals in life. Vastly different.

It was still just lust, he reassured himself. On both their parts. Still, to take her to Italy with him and romance her in Venice was playing with fire, especially when it came to *her* feelings. Women loved that kind of thing.

But it was no use. He wanted to do it. Wanted to see the pleasure in her eyes.

So he ignored the risk and sent her a text telling her to cancel his original first-class booking ASAP and to book two business-class seats for them on the same flight, or an equivalent one.

Will do, she texted back.

Ten minutes later, she texted him the details of their flight, at which point he gave in and rang her.

They talked for close to an hour.

CHAPTER EIGHTEEN

'OH, THIS IS HEAVENLY!' Harriet exclaimed once they settled into their business-class seats, Alex insisting Harriet have the window seat, with him right beside her.

It was early evening on the Monday, take-off in ten minutes. Only one brief stopover, in Dubai, then straight on to Malpensa airport, where they would arrive on Tuesday midmorning, Milan time.

'Thank you, Alex,' she said, turning her head to look over at him.

'For what? You paid for your own ticket.' He was still slightly exasperated with her over that. He'd wanted to spoil her. Make her feel special. Make up to her for what her mean and disgustingly unfair father had done. She'd told him a few more details about her father's appalling treatment last night. It had made him so angry, he'd felt like driving up to Singleton and teaching the man a lesson. When questioned about her mother, Harriet had also confessed that she sent her mother birthday and Mother's Day cards every year, with money enclosed, but never received a reply. How heartbreaking was that?

'Thank you for persuading me to come with you,' she said with the loveliest smile.

He reached over and took her hand in his. 'My pleasure,' he said softly.

Once again, Harriet's heart turned over and this time she noticed. For a split second she started worrying that she was falling in love with Alex, but just as quickly she decided to ignore any such worry. What would be, would be. She wasn't going to spoil this trip by stressing over future complications. She was going to have fun. And live in the moment.

A flight attendant materialised by their seats, with a tray holding glasses of champagne.

'Champagne, sir? Madam?' he asked.

'The lady doesn't drink champagne,' Alex replied.

'Can I get you anything else, sir? Some white wine, perhaps?'

'When will you be serving dinner?'

'About half an hour after take-off.'

'We'll have a bottle of wine with our meals. Perhaps some juice for now. What kind, Harriet?'

'I prefer orange,' she replied.

'Orange juice for two,' Alex relayed.

'Very good, sir. I'll be back shortly.'

Harriet loved the way Alex took command of situations. It had been sweet of him to remember about the champagne, and very sweet of him to insist on coming to pick her up today when it had been really out of his way. She could just have easily caught a taxi. She was glad she hadn't; his authoritative presence defused her tension over the trip, replacing anxiety with excitement, especially after he'd reassured her that everything was under control at the office. She had momentarily contemplated telling Emily about her affair with Alex. But only momentarily. She didn't want Emily to say anything negative or critical.

Of course, it was probably silly of her to have let Alex persuade her to accompany him to Italy. Nothing could come of it. Nothing except…

Harriet brought herself up short before she could start thinking of the future again. Instead, she concentrated on the plusses of her affair with Alex. After all, how could she possibly regret having him as her lover? He was incredibly good in bed; last weekend had been the most amazing experience of her life. He was good out of bed, too, proving to be a fun companion, nothing at all like his often serious persona at work. As for this trip... Harriet vowed to enjoy every single moment. The prospect of spending more time alone with Alex was exciting enough, but to spend that time with him in stunning places like Lake Como and Venice was almost too good to be true. She had to keep glancing over at him to remind herself that it *was* true.

'Yes?' he queried after she'd probably looked at him one time too many.

'Nothing. Just checking that you're real.'

The steward arrived with the orange juice, relieving Harriet of having to explain her rather cryptic remark. It was freshly squeezed juice, and deliciously chilled, just the way she liked it. Harriet sipped it and sighed.

'I don't think I'll ever be able to fly anything but business class from now on,' she said.

'That can be arranged,' Alex said. 'I was thinking of taking you to Rio during our Christmas break.'

Harriet's heart skipped a beat at the thought that he was planning so far ahead. Christmas was five months away. As much as she was tempted just to say yes to anything he suggested, she could not afford to let him think she would settle for being his secret mistress for the rest of her life.

Her smile was light. 'What happened to the Alex who said I should just live for the here and now?'

'He was a fraud. And an opportunist. I've always been a planner, Harry. Just like you.'

'Well, that's a shame. Because I think that that particular Alex might have had the right idea. I've always worried too much about the future. Always planned too much. And where did it get me in the end? Nowhere.'

'I don't know about that, Harry. You have a nice flat near Bondi Beach, money in the bank, the best boss in the world and an even better lover.'

She had to laugh. 'You *are* an arrogant devil.' Not to mention so handsome that every woman on this plane had craned to look at him as they boarded. Harriet had felt so proud to be the woman by his side, resolving to wallow in the experience whilst it lasted.

It was the lasting part, however, that kept coming back to haunt her. Harriet knew in her heart that by Christmas this would all be over. Oh, dear, she was doing it again. Worrying about the future.

The thought sent a sad sigh escaping her lungs.

'You do that a lot, you know,' Alex said.

'Do what?'

'Sigh.'

'Sorry.'

'No need to apologise. It's just that I sometimes wonder what's behind the sigh.'

'Nothing serious. It's just a habit of mine, a way of relieving tension.'

'You're afraid of flying?'

Afraid of flying and dying and falling in love with the wrong man. Again.

'A little,' she admitted.

'Then here…take my hand. We're about to take off.'

Alex took her hand and squeezed it tight, feeling the tension in her as the jumbo airbus zoomed along the wet runway—it had started to rain—before lifting into the air slowly but safely. When the jet levelled off at God knew what height, she sighed again, then took her hand out of his. Alex wished she hadn't. He'd liked holding her hand.

When Alex sighed, Harriet leant over and poked him. '*You're* doing it now.'

He sent her a droll look. 'Maybe it's catching.'

'Maybe you're not the big, brave boy you pretend to be.'

'I never pretend, Harry. I don't like flying, but I'm not scared of it. What's the worst that can happen? The plane crashes and you die. There are worse ways to go.'

Harriet nodded, her big brown eyes turning soft. 'You're thinking of your mother, aren't you?'

Despite the sympathetic note in her voice, Alex could not stop his heart from hardening at the memory of what that wonderful woman had suffered. And so unnecessarily. It had blighted him, knowing he could do nothing to ease her pain. He'd been holding her hand when she'd taken her last breath. He could still see the look on his father's face when he realised she had gone. Poor bastard. Hopefully, this time he'd stick with the rehab and get his life back on track. When he'd rung him earlier today, he'd sounded good.

'Or is it your dad you're worrying about?' Harriet asked.

Her intuition touched him. 'Not really. You were right the first time. I was thinking of my mother.'

He glanced over at Harriet and smiled. 'But let's not talk about sad things. We're off to Italy, to beautiful Lake Como and then on to amazing Venice, which, I might add, I have never seen.'

Harriet's eyes lit up with surprise. 'You haven't?'

'Nope. It will be the first time for both of us. I've been to Lake Como, of course. Jeremy and I holidayed with Sergio at his family villa quite a lot over the years.'

'You three are very close, aren't you?'

'Yep. Have been since our Oxford days.'

'Which is where you all joined that Bachelor's Club.'

'We didn't join it. We *formed* it. There were just the three of us. But that's ancient history now. In reality, the Bachelor's Club is no more. Once Sergio turned thirty-five, he decided to get married, so that was virtually the end of it.'

'What did his turning thirty-five have to do with it?'

'That was the age we vowed to stay bachelors till. And the age we aimed to become billionaires by.'

'Heavens. And did you? Become billionaires, I mean?'

Alex hesitated to tell her, out of habit. He'd always kept the extent of his wealth a secret, well aware that having heaps of money sometimes brought out the worst in people. Men envied and women grovelled. He quickly realised, however, that Harriet was not that type of woman. He'd never met a more independent, less grovelling female in his life.

'Yes, we did,' he admitted.

'*All* of you?'

Clearly, she was taken aback. Alex smiled, both at her and the memory of how their financial goals had finally been reached. Though just in time.

'It took many years, of course,' he explained. 'You don't become a billionaire overnight.'

'I would imagine not. So how *did* it happen?'

'Shortly after we started the Bachelor's Club,

the three of us went into partnership in a wine bar. It was basically a dump, but the location was good. Very close to the university and between two restaurants. We worked hard to turn it into a hip and happening place. At least, Sergio and I worked hard. Jeremy provided the money. He was the wealthy one in our group. Anyway, to cut a long story short, we didn't stop at one wine bar. We eventually had several, all done out the same way. In the end, they were so successful that we formed a franchise. That was how we became billionaires. A little while ago, we sold the WOW franchise to an American company.'

'Oh, my goodness!' Harriet exclaimed. 'You owned the WOW wine bars? That's amazing! Emily and I go to the one in town all the time. They're so cool.'

'They are indeed. But we didn't own any of them in the end. We sold the ones we originally owned years ago. We just owned the franchise.'

'So, that's what you were doing in London recently? Selling the franchise?'

'Yes.'

'I did wonder what business interests you had over there.'

'Well, now you know.'

Harriet fell silent for a long moment before turning to look at him. 'Do you mind if I ask why you three boys decided to stay bachelors in the first place? I mean, I know most men these days don't rush to the altar, but they usually want to settle down eventually. It seems strange that all three of you wanted to stay single so much that you actually formed a club.'

'Look, it was just a bit of fun to begin with. We were all pretty sloshed at the time. Though underneath the fun we all had some serious reasons for embracing bachelorhood. Sergio was still bitter over his father marrying a gold-digger. Jeremy was anti-marriage due to the number of divorces in his family. As for myself... I'd vowed on my mother's deathbed to spend my life making enough money to make sure no one had to suffer what my family did. Making that sort of money—and making a difference—is hard. I didn't see myself ever having the time or the energy to marry and have children of my own. Remaining a bachelor suited my goals.'

Or, it *had*...

Alex could not ignore the fact that he'd reached

his goals now. So maybe it was time to change his mind about staying a bachelor. Maybe it was time to face his inner demons and admit to himself that all he'd just said to Harriet was just rubbish. The truth was, he was afraid of falling in love. Afraid of ending up like his pathetic father.

It was a crazy fear. Irrational, really. Other than in looks, he was nothing like his father. But fear was not always logical.

He gazed into Harriet's lovely face and wished he could be more like Sergio. Fearless and brave when it came to matters of the heart. But he was more like Jeremy, tainted by life's negative experiences, wary of feeling anything too deeply.

'What are you thinking?' she asked.

'Just how lovely you are,' he returned.

Her smile was wry. 'You shouldn't lie to me, Alex. You weren't thinking that at all.'

'You're right. I was thinking that it's rather sad that the Bachelor's Club is no longer relevant. It was a seriously fun club to belong to.'

'No doubt. But I think your Bachelor's Club is past its use-by date, Alex.'

'Only for one of us, Harry. Jeremy and I will soldier on.'

Her lips pursed. 'I have a feeling I won't like this Jeremy.'

Alex had to smile. 'Yes, you will. *Everyone* likes Jeremy.'

CHAPTER NINETEEN

THE CAPTAIN HAD just announced their descent into Milan when Alex turned to her.

'I didn't want to say anything earlier,' he said. 'I wanted you to enjoy the flight and not stress over anything, but Jeremy is going to meet me at the airport. Whilst I'm in Milan, I'm to be whisked off to some tailoring establishment to have a fitting for my suit for the wedding, after which we have to pick up Sergio at his factory, then drive down to Lake Como together.'

Harriet's heart sank. She didn't want to meet any of his rich friends, especially this Jeremy character.

'But won't that be awkward? How are you going to explain me?'

'I'm not,' he replied. 'We won't leave the plane together. You can go first. I know I said we were going to take the train down to Lake Como together, and I was going to see you safely booked into the hotel before I left you, but that was before Jeremy insisted on meeting me.'

Harriet could feel panic setting in. She was a confident girl travelling by train around Sydney, but to travel alone in a strange country was daunting.

'Stop worrying,' he said, seeing alarm in her face. 'I've booked you a hire car which will take you from the airport to the hotel door. The driver will be waiting for you in arrivals, holding up a card with your name on it. He'll help you with your luggage and so forth. I asked for a driver who spoke good English so that you wouldn't feel uncomfortable. Now, stop looking at me like that.'

'Like what?'

'Like I'm abandoning you in a strange land.'

'Sorry. I know it's not your fault.'

'I'll ring you when I can. Or text you if I can't.'

'All right,' she said and sighed.

'And stop that damn sighing,' he snapped. 'You could have come to the wedding with me, but you refused.'

'I wouldn't have fitted in.'

'Rubbish. It's not too late to change your mind, you know. Come with me. Be with me.'

'But what about the hire car? And the booking at the hotel?'

'Nothing that can't be sorted out.'

'I don't know, Alex. Are you sure?'

Not even remotely, he thought. But he couldn't bear to see her go off alone, looking unhappy and worried. He'd brought her here. It was his job to look after her.

'Positive,' he said. 'Now, I don't want to hear another word about it. You're coming with me and that's that.'

Her smile did things to him that shouldn't be allowed. Dear God, if he didn't watch himself, he would fall in love with her. And that would never do.

'I'll just go along to the ladies' and freshen up,' she said.

'Better be quick. We'll be landing soon.'

'I'm always quick,' she told him with a wry smile. 'I have a boss who gives me five-minute deadlines all the time.'

'What a bastard.'

'He can be.'

'I'll have to have a word with him.'

'He won't listen. He never listens.'

'Stupid as well.'

She laughed, then left him. He watched her make her way down the aisle, her neat little backside encased in stylish black slacks. She wore black a lot, usually teaming it with white tops. Harriet's top today was a simple but expensive-looking white T-shirt. He watched her walk back towards him five minutes later, her dark hair swinging in a sleek curtain around her shoulders, her glossy red lipstick a perfect foil for her black-and-white outfit. Though not classically beautiful, Harriet's face was strikingly attractive, her big dark eyes her best feature.

'That's better,' she said as she sat down and clicked her seat belt into place. 'Can't have your best friends looking down their noses at me.'

'They'll love you,' he said, confident that neither Sergio nor Jeremy would make any girlfriend of his feel bad. Which was exactly how he would introduce Harriet. Not as his PA. As his new girlfriend. Jeremy wouldn't care that he was sleeping with one of his staff, but Sergio might.

Alex tried to remember if he'd ever told his friends his relatively new PA's name. He vaguely recalled saying something about her the last night they'd had dinner together a few weeks ago. Yes, he'd called her Harry, Jeremy having picked up that that was probably a nickname. Sergio, however, had been very distracted that night, his mind clearly on Bella. He was unlikely to remember what his PA was called.

Alex decided to clue Jeremy in on who Harriet really was, but he would keep Sergio in the dark. He wasn't in the mood for any lectures where his private life was concerned, especially from Sergio, who was stupidly about to marry a possible gold-digger!

The plane's landing was as smooth as silk, their disembarking just as trouble-free. They were whisked through Customs without a hitch, Alex collecting and loading their luggage on a trolley before proceeding to the arrivals area, an anxious-looking Harriet by his side.

Jeremy, as luck would have it, was standing not that far from a uniformed chauffeur who was holding up a card with Harriet's name on it. It wasn't till that moment that Alex thought of a way to soothe some of Harriet's nervousness over having to spend too much time with his friends.

'Jeremy! Mate!' he called out and steered Harriet in his direction.

CHAPTER TWENTY

JEREMY WASN'T ANYTHING like Harriet had been imagining. Since Alex virtually had described him as the best-dressed rake in London, she'd pictured a handsome but dissolute-looking man with slicked-back hair and heavy-lidded eyes, wearing a designer suit and sporting a lot of expensive jewellery.

The man who waved back at Alex *was* handsome, but he looked disgustingly healthy with a nice tan and sparkling blue eyes. His hair wasn't oily or slicked back. It was clearly freshly washed, brown and collar-length, with a boyish wave which fell across his high forehead. As for his clothes...they looked expensive but were very casual. Not a bit of jewellery, either, Harriet noted as they drew closer. No earrings or rings or even a watch.

When he threw his arms around Alex in a huge bear hug, Harriet was astounded, then oddly touched. It wasn't often that you saw grown men hug each other with such genuine warmth and affection.

'God, it's great to see you,' Jeremy said at the same time, astounding Harriet even more with the richness and depth of his voice, which seemed at odds with his size. Though far from short—he was only a couple of inches shorter than Alex—his frame was much leaner. His shoulders were broad enough, but the rest of his body was very slender. He could easily have made money as a model, or as a narrator, with that gorgeous voice of his.

Harriet couldn't remember what he did for a living. She didn't think Alex had actually told her. Just that he was a rich friend from Oxford and was a fellow member of their Bachelor's Club, which meant he, too, had recently become a billionaire. He *looked* rich; money had a way of clinging to a man like an invisible cloak.

When he cheekily winked at Harriet over Alex's shoulder, she got a glimpse of his much-vaunted charm.

'So, who's this gorgeous creature, Alex?' he asked as he stepped back to look her up and down, his blue eyes twinkling. 'You never mentioned you were bringing someone with you.'

'It was a last-minute decision. This is Harriet,' Alex introduced. 'My PA. And my new girlfriend,' he added before Harriet could be offended. 'I usually call her Harry, but in present company I think Harriet is called for.'

She saw the drily amused look Jeremy gave Alex. 'You sneaky devil,' he said, then grinned. 'And you had the hide to tell me that business and pleasure don't mix!'

'There are exceptions to every rule,' Alex said and smiled a wry smile at a slightly startled Harriet. 'I didn't say anything because I agreed to keep our affair a secret. But there's no need for secrets over here, though I think I might not tell Sergio she's my PA. Sergio isn't as much of a free spirit as you are, Jeremy. Without going into too many details, I have to speak to that chauffeur over there. He was going to drive Harriet down to a hotel at Lake Como, but I've persuaded her to change her plans and come to the wedding with me.'

'And rightly so,' Jeremy pronounced warmly as Alex walked off, leaving Harriet to fend alone in his friend's perversely bewitching company. It was simply impossible not to like him. She wasn't sexually attracted to him, but she could understand why lots of women had fallen under his spell over the years. He possessed a personal charisma which she imagined could be overpowering if he was also your physical type.

'It's wonderful to see Alex dating a real woman for a change,' he said. 'Though slightly disconcerting.'

'Disconcerting?'

'I don't want to be the only one left a bachelor in our Bachelor's Club. Oops. Maybe I shouldn't have said that. Has Alex told you about the Bachelor's Club?'

'Yes. I know all about it.'

'That's a relief. Thought I'd put my big foot in it just then. Sergio's broken ranks, but Alex and I are still committed bachelors. We both believe it's best for a girl to know the lie of the land before she gets in too deep. Or is it too late for that?' he added with a sudden searching look.

Oh, God. Why did she have to blush?

'I see,' he said, his brows drawing together.

'No, you don't,' she said quickly. 'Look, I know

Alex isn't into love or marriage. I'm not a fool. I recently broke up with my fiancé and I'm not looking for love or commitment of any kind. I'm just having a much-needed fling. It won't last. When it's over, I'll move on and so will Alex.'

'Are you quite sure about that?'

'Quite sure,' she said coolly and glanced over at Alex, who was still talking to the chauffeur. Just then, he glanced back at her, smiled, then hurried over, the chauffeur in his wake.

'Right. All settled. Jeremy, am I right in guessing you didn't drive yourself to the airport? Knowing you, you either had Sergio drop you off or you took a taxi.'

'I hate it when people know me that well,' he said, but without looking offended at all. 'Yes, Sergio dropped me off, then went on to his office. He's getting everything organised there before he and Bella fly off to New York.'

'Thought that might be the case,' Alex said. 'Anyway, I've organised for Lucca here to take us all to the tailor. After we're finished there, we'll drop you off back at Sergio's office, Jeremy, then I'll accompany Harriet down to the hotel I booked her into on Lake Como. Everyone, this is Lucca,' he finally introduced. 'Lucca, this is Harriet and Jeremy.'

Relief swamped Harriet at Alex not insisting that she stay at Sergio's villa on Lake Como. Now that she'd met Jeremy, she wasn't quite so nervous about meeting Sergio—whom she was sure would be nice to her as well—but she didn't want to spend every minute of the next two days in their company. Besides, it was only natural that the three friends would like to spend some time together. Clearly, that didn't happen too often these days.

'I'll tell you what,' Harriet butted in before he could put his plans into motion. 'Why don't you and Jeremy take a taxi to wherever it is you have to go and I'll have Lucca take me straight down to the hotel? To be honest,' she added, 'I feel seriously jet-lagged. You're an experienced traveller, Alex, but I'm not. I hardly slept a wink on that flight. Now, please, don't worry about me. I'll be fine. I'm going to go straight to bed once I check in, and sleep for hours, so don't go calling me for ages. Tonight'll be soon enough.'

'Are you sure?' Alex asked.

'Absolutely. I'm quite capable of looking after

myself, like we originally planned. Go have some fun with your friends.'

He leant forward and gave her a peck on the cheek. 'You're a darling.'

His sweet words sent tears pricking at her eyes.

'Off you go,' she said hurriedly before she could embarrass herself totally. 'Lucca will look after me, won't you, Lucca?'

Lucca, who was a good-looking lad of no more than twenty, nodded enthusiastically. '*Si*. You will be safe with me.'

'Safe' was not quite the word Harriet would have used to describe Lucca's driving. Thankfully, the road from Milan to Lake Como was first class, but good God, didn't they have speed limits in Italy? If they did, Lucca was oblivious to them. Once off the freeway, fortunately he did slow down enough for Harriet to take in the sights. And what sights they were! Never had she seen such a beautiful spot as Lake Como, with its surrounding snow-capped mountains and magnificent villa-dotted shores.

The boutique hotel they were heading for was once a private villa, according to its website. The pictures of it looked beautiful, and the setting peaceful, which was why she'd booked it. But flat, one-dimensional photographs did not replicate the experience of seeing the place in real life, Harriet was soon to appreciate, especially on a warm summer's day with a clear blue sky.

When the hotel came into view, she was overwhelmed by the sheer grandeur of the ancient stone building gleaming a soft white in the sunshine. The magnificence of the grounds and the view of the lake were just as spellbinding. Harriet's eyes were everywhere as she followed Lucca into the grand foyer with its vaulted ceiling and spectacular marble staircase. She'd been in some nice hotels in Sydney over the years, but there was nothing at home like this. It was like stepping back in time to a world of splendour, elegance and opulent luxury, a feeling enhanced when she finally lay down on her antique four-poster bed in her exquisitely furnished room.

She didn't really want to go to sleep just yet. She wanted to wander in the garden and sit on the terrace which overlooked the lake. Instead, the excitement of the trip and the length of the flight finally caught up with her and she couldn't stop herself from drifting off, her last thought being that she hoped Alex was enjoying himself.

Alex finally became aware of the fact that Jeremy had been uncharacteristically quiet during their trip to the tailor. After the fitting was finished, Alex suggested they go have a spot of lunch somewhere. He was curious about what was bothering Jeremy. He suspected it was something to do with Harriet; Alex wondered what she'd said to him that had rendered him unusually taciturn.

They found a café nearby which wasn't too crowded. Summer in Milan was high tourist season, with all the cafés and restaurants doing excellent business. Alex had by then removed his suit jacket and rolled up his sleeves, but he was still on the warm side. Fortunately, the café was air-conditioned.

'Okay, so what's bugging you?' Alex asked after the waitress had departed with their order of wraps and coffee.

Jeremy widened ingenuous blue eyes. 'Why would you think something's bugging me?'

'Don't try to con me, Jeremy. I know you, re-member?'

Jeremy shrugged. 'Okay, but you might not like what I have to say.'

'Let me be the judge of that.'

'Are you in love with this girl, Alex?'

His question stunned Alex. It was certainly not what he'd been expecting.

'No,' he said. 'I'm not.' Not yet, anyway.

'I see.' Jeremy began making circles on the table with his index finger, an old habit of his when he was thinking. Finally, he stopped and looked up at Alex. 'Harriet told me she's not in-terested in love or commitment from you. She says she's having a fling on the rebound.'

Alex only just contained his exasperation. 'I leave you with her for five minutes and she tells you her innermost thoughts and feelings. How on earth did you manage that?'

'It's a talent I inherited,' Jeremy said with a perfect poker face. 'All the Barker-Whittle males are born charmers. But that's beside the point.'

'And the point is?'

'I know you very well, Alex, the same way you know me. It's not like you to become involved with an employee, especially your PA. You're nothing like me. You have hidden depths. And a capacity for caring which I simply don't possess.'

'Don't undersell yourself, dear friend. You have a great capacity for caring. Look how you always remember everyone's birthdays.'

'Stop trying to be funny, Alex. This is serious.'

'What is?'

Jeremy's blue eyes turned a steely grey. 'I have this awful feeling that you're heading for an even worse disaster than Sergio's marriage.'

'In what way?'

'I'm worried you're going to fall in love with this girl and she's going to break your heart.'

Alex was taken aback. 'I can't see that happening.'

Jeremy shook his head. 'This is not going to end well, Alex.'

'Everything will work out fine, Jeremy. Harry and I are just having a bit of fun together. Lighten up, for pity's sake. It's not like you to worry so much.'

Jeremy heaved a frustrated sigh. 'You're right. I'm in danger of becoming a worrywart. And a workaholic. Ever since I bought my book business, I've changed.'

'I didn't notice much of a change when I rang you the other night,' Alex pointed out drily. 'You were happily bedding your French editor with your usual *laissez-faire* attitude. Ah…our wraps are here.'

Both men tucked into the food and didn't speak for a couple of minutes.

'I do know what you mean about changing, though,' Alex went on finally. 'I've changed, too, this past year. Possibly it's because we're getting older. Just think, both you and I will be thirty-five before the year is out. I hope we'll always stay friends, despite the tyranny of distance, but our lives are now taking different paths.'

'God, that sounds wretched. I already miss you and Sergio both. Terribly.'

Alex was touched by his words, but not surprised. Of the three friends, Jeremy had always been the softest, and the most sentimental. He *never* forgot birthdays. It came to Alex that Jeremy's *laissez-faire* attitude to life might hide a deep-seated loneliness. His upbringing, though privileged, had not been easy. He'd been sent to boarding school when he was eight, where his slight frame and pretty-boy looks had resulted in lots of bullying. It wasn't till puberty had hit that he'd found his feet, his voice breaking and his height shooting up to over six feet, putting paid to the bullying. But his less than positive experiences at school, plus his parents' constant divorcing and remarrying, had left lots of emotional scars.

'Who knows?' Alex said casually. 'Maybe *you'll* fall in love one day.'

'What?'

Alex laughed. 'You should see the look on your face.'

'Well, it isn't every day that one of my best friends says something to me so outrageous. I would possibly tolerate it from Sergio, now that he's about to embrace wedded bliss. But I expected better from a fellow dedicated bachelor.'

'I was only joking. Come on, finish up that coffee. Then we'll go pick up Sergio.'

Dragging Sergio away from work was not an easy task, but Jeremy managed it when he promised to tell Sergio some fascinating news, but only once they were on their way to Lake Como.

Alex knew exactly what he had in mind, but went along with it. After all, if he was going to bring Harriet to the wedding, Sergio had to know about her.

'Okay, out with it!' an impatient Sergio demanded within thirty seconds of leaving the factory. Jeremy leant forward from where he was sitting in the back seat, kindly having given Alex the passenger seat.

'Alex brought a girl with him. No, no, strike that. He brought a *woman*.'

Sergio shot Alex a surprised look. 'A woman, eh? What happened?'

'I finally grew bored with dating dolly-birds whose IQs were smaller than their bra size.'

Jeremy chuckled. 'That's a good one, Alex.'

'So how did you meet this woman?' Sergio asked.

'Through work. She's in real estate.' He'd instructed Jeremy not to mention she was his PA.

'What's her name?' Sergio asked.

'Harriet.'

'Classy name.'

'She's a classy girl.'

'I thought she was a woman.'

'She is. But she's not that old. Late twenties.'

'Around Bella's age, then. I presume she's attractive.'

'*Very* attractive,' Jeremy jumped in. 'Brunette. Slim. She's also nicely independent. I met her at the airport.'

'So where the hell *is* she?' Sergio asked.

'By now she's settled in at the Villa Accorsi. You know it?'

'Of course. But why is she staying at a hotel when we have plenty of room at my place?'

'She didn't want to stay there. To be honest, she didn't even want to come to the wedding, but I talked her into it.'

'Are you serious about this Harriet?'

'Silly question, Sergio,' Jeremy intoned drily. 'Alex is never serious about *any* girl.'

'But it's clear this one is different. He wouldn't have brought her all this way if he didn't at least like her a hell of a lot.'

'I do like her a hell of a lot,' Alex confessed. 'But we've only been dating a short while. She's also just getting over a broken engagement. When Harry told me she'd always wanted to go to Italy, I impulsively asked her along—something I'll start to regret if my friends start harassing me over my intentions.'

When Sergio fell broodingly silent, Alex worried that he might have come down a bit heavy.

'Look, I'm sorry, I—'

'It's your PA you should apologise to,' Sergio broke in sharply. 'Did you honestly think I wouldn't remember? You called her Harry that night at dinner a few weeks back. The odds of both your new girlfriend and your PA being called Harry are at lotto-winning level, so let's cut the crap and tell the truth. You're having sex with your personal assistant—most likely on the sly—and you're using this trip as an excuse to have some more.'

Alex sighed heavily, whilst Jeremy remained conspicuously silent, both of them having been on the end of Sergio's disapproval more than once over the years.

'It's not like that,' Alex said defensively.

'Then what's it like?'

'We're just having some fun together. It's nothing serious.'

Jeremy's snort didn't help.

'Harry needs some fun right now,' Alex went on firmly. 'I would never hurt her.'

Now Sergio snorted.

Alex decided he'd heard enough. 'Hey, just cut it with the "high and mighty" stuff, buddy. From what I've heard, your intentions weren't exactly pure as the driven snow when you invited Bella to stay at your villa.'

Sergio had the grace to apologise.

'I was just thinking,' Jeremy piped up. 'We should have your stag party tonight. That way we won't be hung over for the wedding. What do you say, Sergio?'

'I say good thinking. I still have half a case of that gorgeous red you sent me last Christmas.'

'Great. And we'll order in some of those fantastic pizzas we ate last time. You like pizza, don't you, Alex?'

'I like good pizza.'

'These are the best. So that's settled. Another bonus is it leaves Alex free to spend tomorrow to do some sightseeing with Harriet. He could even stay the night with her. Then they can come to the wedding together the next morning.'

'You'd better watch it, Jeremy,' Alex said. 'You're turning into a planner.'

'You could be right,' he agreed. 'Like I told you, since I bought my book business I seem to have developed a strange compulsion for being organised. When I was working for the family bank, I didn't give a damn about nine-to-five, or even turning up at my desk at all. I did most of my business via my phone. Now I'm getting obsessed with marketing meetings and publishing deadlines and all sorts of weird things.'

Both Sergio and Alex laughed.

'We'll make a businessman out of him yet,' Alex said.

'Stranger things have happened, I suppose,' Jeremy remarked.

'About tomorrow night,' Sergio piped up. 'With the wedding at eleven, I'd be more comfortable if you spent that night with us at my place, Alex. I don't want anything going wrong.'

'Fair enough,' Alex said. 'How will Harriet get to the wedding, then?'

'I'll book her a water taxi to pick her up at the hotel around ten. They have their own jetty.'

'Okay.' Alex didn't mind. He would have all

day with her, more than enough time to show her some sights *and* have late-afternoon delight in her hotel room. He wondered what Harriet was doing right at this moment. Hopefully, she was having a good rest and not feeling lonely or abandoned. He would call her later. Or perhaps he would just text her; tell her they were having their stag party tonight and that he would join her tomorrow morning. Yes, perhaps that would be better. He didn't want her thinking he simply *had* to hear the sound of her voice.

CHAPTER TWENTY-ONE

WHEN HARRIET WOKE, she wasn't sure where she was for a split second. But then she remembered. She was in Italy, in a gorgeous hotel on the shores of Lake Como.

Unfortunately, she was also alone. Harriet pulled a face. What she would not give to have Alex by her side at this moment.

Thinking of Alex had her rolling over, picking up her phone and turning it back on. Good Lord! It was almost seven o'clock. She'd slept for hours. She hoped he hadn't tried to ring her. She quickly checked. No. No missed calls, but one message, informing her that they were having Sergio's stag party that night so that they wouldn't be hung over for the wedding. This would also leave tomorrow free for him to spend with her.

Harriet's spirits immediately lifted.

'Ring me when you wake up,' he'd added before signing off.

She did so straight away, just the sound of his voice filling her with joy.

'Did you have a good sleep?' he asked.

'Very good.'

They talked for ages, Alex telling her of all the places he planned to take her the next day. Sergio had offered the use of his speedboat. It sounded wonderful. Still, she would enjoy going anywhere with Alex.

'Hey!' She heard a deep male voice call out. Jeremy, no doubt. He did have a distinctive voice.

'Girlfriends aren't allowed at stag parties,' he said. 'Not even via the phone.'

Harriet's heart turned over at the word 'girl-friend'. It sounded wonderful as well, though she'd better not get used to it. That would only be her title here, in this fantasy world, on this fantasy getaway. Once they got back to the real world at home, she would revert to being Alex's PA, plus his secret bit on the side.

It was a depressing thought.

Then don't think about that, Harriet, she lectured herself. *Live in the moment*. That was the order of the day.

'I'd better go,' Alex said. 'See you tomorrow morning around nine-thirty.'

'That early?'

'Don't worry. I won't be drinking too much. I'll leave that up to Sergio and Jeremy. I'll give you a call when I'm on my way. Bye, sweetheart.'

That evening seemed endless, despite the excellence of the meal she had in a local restaurant. She kept thinking about Alex, then about tomorrow. She could hardly wait.

She woke very early the next day, already excited. Unfortunately, it was still over three hours before Alex was due to join her. Showering, dressing and titivating took up a good hour and a half, and Harriet used up another hour having a leisurely breakfast out on the huge back terrace that overlooked the lake. The day promised to be warm again, but not too warm, with a smattering of cloud in the sky. She was lingering over a third cup of coffee when her phone pinged. Snatching it up, she read the message from Alex with a pounding heart.

I'm on my way, it said. Be on the lookout for the boat. It's red, so it should be easy to spot.

Harriet stood up and made her way over to

stand at the stone railing that enclosed the terrace. Her eyes scanned the lake, looking for a red speedboat. There were myriad assorted craft on the water. Ferries, water taxis, sailing boats, jet skis and, yes, several speedboats, none of them red.

And then she saw it, cutting across the wake of a ferry, jumping the waves, Alex at the wheel, his fair hair glinting golden in the sunshine. He arrived like a hero from an action movie, Harriet only then noticing the hotel jetty at the bottom of some stone steps. Spotting her watching him from the terrace, he waved, jumped out of the boat, tied a rope around a post, then dashed up the steps towards her, dashingly handsome in white shorts and a navy polo. He gathered her to him and kissed her thoroughly, uncaring of the other guests sitting at tables nearby. When he finally let her come up for air, Harriet didn't care, either.

'You're looking good for a man who should have a hangover,' she said, cupping his face and pretending to inspect his eyes. Lord, but he had beautiful eyes, blue as the sky overhead, and with lashes that any woman would kill for.

'I told you I wouldn't drink much.'

'Have you had breakfast?'

'Would you believe that I have? Maria insisted on cooking an omelette.'

'Who's Maria?'

'Sergio's housekeeper. She wanted to pack me a picnic lunch, but I said no to that. So, are you ready to go? First, we're going over to Bellagio. You can't visit Lake Como without visiting the town of Bellagio. It's called "the pearl of Lake Como".'

'Sounds lovely.'

'It is. Very old, of course, but fascinating. Seeing all the main places of interest there will take us all morning. We'll have lunch there, too. Their restaurants are second to none. Then after lunch we'll motor down to Como. That's a beautiful town. After that I'll take you for a leisurely drive around the whole lake. You can see a lot from the water. I'll show you Sergio's villa, plus the one next door, the countess's. It's very grand. That's where they're having the wedding and the reception afterwards.'

'It's not going to be a big wedding, is it?'

Alex laughed. 'Hardly. Counting the celebrant and the photographer, there'll be just eleven of us. So don't start stressing that it's some huge celebrity shindig, because it isn't.'

Harriet had to admit she was relieved. She hadn't packed a dress suitable for a seriously formal do. But she *had* brought along her red cocktail dress, the one Alex had admired. That would do.

'Now, are you ready to go? You look ready. And you look very lovely, might I add. If I hadn't had our itinerary all worked out, I'd whisk you off upstairs for a quickie.'

'I don't much like quickies,' Harriet said, doing her best to ignore the wild jab of desire coursing through her veins.

He chuckled. 'You are such a little liar. I'm almost tempted to show you just how much. But I think I'll make you wait.'

'I can wait,' she told him. 'Provided you give me a little taster occasionally.'

'And what would that involve?'

'Nothing much. Just hold my hand and kiss me at regular intervals so that I don't go cold on you.'

'Done!'

* * *

Alex hadn't enjoyed himself so much in years. He'd been to Lake Como a few times as Sergio's guest, and he'd seen the various sights on offer, but there was something about seeing them through Harriet's delighted eyes which made the experience even more pleasurable, and infinitely more satisfying. Of course, it didn't hurt holding her hand or kissing her more times than he could count. By the time they docked at the hotel jetty in the late afternoon, he was more than ready to steer her up the amazing staircase to her room without further ado.

She made no objection to sharing a shower with him, or having what turned out to be a quickie under the jets of hot water, Alex coming with a speed that bothered him a bit, knowing that Harriet had been left panting and unsatisfied. Still, he made it up to her afterwards with an hour of leisurely love-play in bed, during which she came three times before he reached for a condom once more.

'Hate to love you and leave you,' he said afterwards, 'but I don't want to drive that boat across the lake at night. Sergio is a nervous enough bridegroom without my adding to his worries, so I promised I'd be back before dark.'

Harriet propped herself up on one elbow and watched him dress.

'How am I getting to the wedding?' she asked.

'Sergio's booked you a water taxi for ten. It'll bring you to his villa. I'll meet you down at his jetty and we'll all go over to the countess's place together.'

'I still can't believe how amazing her place is. I mean, Sergio's villa was grand enough, but hers is like a palace.'

'It *is* magnificent, but it's not as big as it looks. The setting up against the hillside makes it look larger.'

When Harriet reached for her phone and took a photo of him, he groaned. 'Will you stop doing that? You've already taken heaps of photos of me today.'

'Yes, but none with your shirt off.'

'I hope none of them shows up on social media,' he warned her.

Harriet shrugged. 'I'm not into social media on a personal basis. It has its uses, but I don't partic-

ularly want to give other people—even friends—
a blow-by-blow description of my life.'

'Sensible girl. But, to be on the safe side, perhaps you'd better not take any snaps at the wedding tomorrow. Sergio has a passion for privacy.'

'In that case, he shouldn't be marrying Bella,
should he?'

Alex laughed. 'You could be right there. Okay,
I'll reassure Sergio that any photos you take are
for your personal use only. They won't be grac-
ing the glossies, or anywhere else.'

Harriet smiled. 'Good. Because I really want
to take some photos. Not just of the bride. I especially want one of you and your two friends
together.'

Alex bent down and gave her a kiss on the
cheek. 'I'd like that. Have to go now, Harry. Sorry
I wasn't able to take you out to dinner tonight.'

'No worries. I'll have room service, then read
one of the books I downloaded onto my tablet
back home before I left.'

'What kind of books?'

'Mostly thrillers, with a few romances thrown
in. What do you suggest I try?'

'Not a romance. Romancing you is *my* job.'

'And you're very good at it, too. Lord knows what I'm going to do when you grow bored and don't want to have sex with me any more. I'm already seriously addicted to your unique brand of lovemaking.'

'I wouldn't worry about that, if I were you,' he said ruefully. 'There's no danger of my growing bored with you for a long time yet.' And wasn't that the truth!

It was actually a relief to hear that Harriet didn't envisage ending their affair any time soon. Alex couldn't bear the thought of her telling him one day that it was over between them. It would happen, of course. She didn't love him. Basically, she was just in it for the sex. Same as him.

Are you sure that's still true, Alex? questioned that inner voice that had been plaguing him ever since Jeremy had brought up the subject of love. *Are you sure that your feelings for her haven't already changed to something far deeper than a combination of liking and lust?*

Alex clenched his jaw down hard, refusing to listen to such rubbish. It was all Jeremy's fault, which was ironic, considering *his* attitude to love and marriage. Alex decided that it was the romantic setting that was making him feel things he didn't normally feel. Paris might be called the city of love, but Italy was the country of love. He would have to watch himself tomorrow at the wedding, and then in Venice. If he wasn't careful, before he knew it he'd be asking Harriet to marry him. Which was pretty stupid, considering he was the last man on earth she would marry. *So just put all these thoughts of love back into Pandora's box, Alex, and get yourself out of here. Pronto!*

'Must fly,' he told her, and with one last peck on the cheek he was gone.

CHAPTER TWENTY-TWO

HARRIET COULD NOT imagine a more perfect wedding. The lack of a church filled to the brim with guests didn't seem to matter, despite her own dream to have that kind of traditional wedding. Or it had been, till she witnessed this one. Admittedly, the setting for the ceremony was idyllic, on the wide stone terrace of a magnificent villa overlooking Lake Como. Plus the weather was beautiful, the skies blue overhead and the summer sun not too hot.

But it was the unique bridal party that dazzled Harriet the most. It wasn't often that there were no bridesmaids, just the bride, groom and two best men. She didn't know whose photograph to take first, they were all so good-looking. The bride, of course, was more than dazzling. Harriet had already known Bella was beautiful. She'd seen her on television and in the gossip magazines. Dressed as a bride, however, she was breathtaking. Yet her gown was simple, a sleek floor-length sheath in pearl satin which skimmed her figure rather than clung. She wore no veil. With that gorgeous mane of white-blonde hair, she didn't need a veil. Her jewellery was just as simple. A fine gold chain with a single pearl pendant, along with pearl-drop earrings.

She and Sergio looked brilliant standing together, his darkly handsome looks the perfect foil for Bella's exquisite blonde beauty. Harriet took heaps of photos, including several of the three friends together. She didn't have an opportunity to meet Bella before the actual ceremony, but Sergio had spoken to her at length as she'd walked with the men from Sergio's villa to the countess's. Such a nice man; a real gentleman. He'd made her feel so welcome, which was good of him, considering she was a wedding crasher.

The countess had been very sweet as well. Her name was Claudia and she was a widow. But a very merry one, Harriet deduced by her flashy clothes and flirtatious manner, especially towards Jeremy. Not that he seemed to mind. Alex had eventually confirmed her suspicions that the two of them might have been lovers at some stage, despite their age difference.

Which didn't surprise Harriet. Nothing would surprise Harriet about Jeremy's behaviour where women were concerned. She even caught him winking at the mother of the bride, who was still attractive and possibly younger than Claudia. The only other guests were Sergio's housekeeper, Maria, and her husband, Carlo, who obviously thought the marriage a marvellous idea, judging by the wide smiles on their faces.

By the time the celebrant—a portly and loquacious Italian named Giovanni—pronounced Sergio and Bella husband and wife, Claudia and the mother of the bride were dabbing at their eyes, though not enough to spoil their make-up.

Harriet felt teary herself, partly because she always cried at weddings, but mostly because she knew she would never marry the man *she* loved. Oh, dear God. She *did* love Alex, didn't she? There was no longer any doubt in her mind. She'd suspected as much yesterday but had pushed the dreaded thought away. When her eyes automatically went to him, more tears threatened. Fortunately, he didn't notice; the official photographer—a tall, thin woman in her forties—had pounced on the bridal party for more photos, leaving Harriet to battle her emotions in private.

Time to get a grip, girl, she lectured herself after slipping her phone back into her black clutch bag. *Go talk to the countess. Or Bella's mother. Whatever, just do something, and for pity's sake, no more silly crying!*

Alex felt impatient for the reception luncheon to be over, despite the happiness of the occasion and the quality of the food. They were sitting at the sumptuous table in Claudia's opulent dining room, being given course after mouth-watering course. Harriet was on his right side and Jeremy on his left, both of them obviously enjoying the lavish meal a lot more than he was. His mind was definitely elsewhere, his gaze drifting over the table to Sergio and Bella, who didn't seem to be eating much. They were too busy gazing adoringly into each other's eyes. Alex finally agreed with Jeremy that Bella did love Sergio; the way she looked at him was rather persuasive. But he would reserve judgment till their marriage had passed the hurdle of Sergio abandoning the family business in order to move to New York with her.

They were actually flying there later this evening, which was the reason for the morning wedding. Knowing this, Alex had booked a hire car to pick both himself and Harriet up at her hotel later that afternoon and take them straight to Venice, where he'd booked them into one of the city's most luxurious hotels. The suite he'd picked had cost a bomb, but he didn't care. He worked hard. Why shouldn't he spoil himself? Alex suspected, however, that it was Harriet whom he wanted to spoil.

He watched her out of the corner of his eye, thinking how lovely she looked today. She was wearing the same red cocktail dress she'd worn to the charity dinner earlier this year, the one which had given him wicked thoughts all that night. Or had they been jealous thoughts? He certainly hadn't liked the thought of her going home with that dullard Dwayne. She'd always deserved someone better.

But you're not better, that annoying voice piped up once again. *Except perhaps in bed. You're selfish and ruthless, and a total waste of time.*

She'd be better off without you in her life. Really, your behaviour has been quite shameless. So do the right thing, Alex, and once you get home let her go.

But he didn't want to let her go. He couldn't. Not yet.

Harriet tried to pretend she was having a wonderful time, but she wasn't. The food was marvellous, yes, but there was way too much of it. The only reason she kept eating was that she didn't want to offend the countess, who'd obviously gone to a lot of trouble to make the wedding a success. She couldn't wait to get out of there and be alone with Alex once more; couldn't wait to go to Venice. Lake Como was lovely, but somehow seeing Sergio and Bella getting married here today had temporarily spoiled the place for her. Venice would be much better. Out of sight was out of mind, or so they said. She didn't want to think about love and marriage. She had to get her mind back to reality, which was that she was having a strictly sexual affair with Alex. Nothing more.

Before she'd left Sydney to come to Italy, Harriet had vowed to enjoy the trip for what it was. But somehow the enjoyment she'd experienced yesterday was in danger of disintegrating. Which was a shame. When she sighed, Alex gave her a nudge.

'None of that infernal sighing,' he muttered under his breath.

Harriet gave him a rueful smile. 'It's just that I'm full,' she whispered. 'I can't eat another bite.'

'Then don't.'

'I won't,' she said and put down her cutlery.

Jeremy leaned forward and shot a questioning glance down the table. 'You don't want your dessert?'

'I'm full,' Harriet answered.

'Pass it along to me. I need added fortification for the night ahead.'

'Don't even ask,' Alex informed her drily as he passed along her dessert.

'He really is very naughty,' Harriet said after Jeremy had dropped them back at the hotel in Sergio's speedboat. The happy couple had by then departed, and Alex wasted no time in getting Jeremy to drive them across the lake. The hire car he'd booked was due to pick them up in less than an hour.

'But you can't help liking him,' she added as they hurried up the steps towards the hotel entrance.

'You don't fancy him, do you?' Alex said, his voice sharp.

'Don't be silly. He's not my type at all.'

'Why not?'

'He just isn't. You're my type, Alex, as you very well know. There's no need to be jealous.'

'I'm not jealous,' he denied. But he was. Fiercely jealous. The thought of Harriet even fancying another man brought a sour taste to his mouth. The thought of her having sex with another man didn't bear thinking about. The only man allowed to have sex with her was *him*!

'How long will it take you to pack?' he asked her.

'Not long. Why?'

He gave her a look which spoke a thousand words. Less than a minute later, Harriet was up against the bedroom door, her panties in tatters on the floor, her legs wrapped around Alex's waist while he pumped up into her with primal passion. As they both came, Alex thanked his lucky stars that he'd had enough foresight to put a condom in his jacket pocket that morning, perhaps anticipating a moment such as this. He shuddered at the thought of what he might have done if he hadn't.

Alex held her close, not wanting to let her go. But he really had to. Time was moving on.

Slowly, gently, he eased out of her, then headed for the bathroom. What he saw there brought a groan of dismay to his lips. Talk about life being cruel. After flushing the toilet, he adjusted his clothes, washed his hands and walked slowly back into the bedroom. Harriet was sitting on the side of the bed, looking slightly dishevelled.

'What is it?' she asked straight away on seeing worry stamped on his face.

'I hate having to tell you this,' he said, his heart sinking, 'but the condom broke.'

'Oh,' she said, then just sat there, silent and thoughtful.

'Is it a dangerous time of the month for you?'

CHAPTER TWENTY-THREE

HARRIET DIDN'T HAVE to think too long to know that it was. Extremely dangerous.

Her first reaction to the possibility of falling pregnant by Alex was despair. If it had been anyone else, she might have had a chance of being happy about having a baby. She'd always wanted to be a mother by the time she was thirty. But she knew having a child would be the last thing *he* wanted.

It took a while for Harriet to see the situation with a calmer mind, but she eventually came to a decision. If she had been unlucky enough to fall pregnant—or lucky enough, depending on how you looked at it—then the problem would be hers.

Finally, she looked up. 'I won't lie to you,' she said. 'There is a chance that I might fall pregnant. It's close to the middle of my cycle. But I also might not. Pregnancies don't always happen, even when people are trying to have a baby. We'll just have to wait and see.' She'd already decided not to tell him if she did. Still, whether she did or not, she was going to resign. She simply could not go on having wildly passionate sex with Alex and pretending it was just lust. She loved the man. But if she told him so, he would dump her cold. Even if it turned out that she wasn't pregnant, how could she continue to work for him under such circumstances? It had all become impossible. Going to Venice with him was impossible, too.

She smothered a sigh and made the hardest decision of her life.

'I'm sorry, Alex, but I can't go to Venice with you. Not now. I just want to go home.'

'But there's no need to do that. We could go buy you one of those morning-after pills. Then you won't have to worry.'

You mean you *won't have to worry*, Harriet thought unhappily. Still, she supposed it was a sensible suggestion and one which she hadn't thought of. Silly, really. It would solve the problem. Though not *all* of her problems.

'I still want to go home, Alex,' she said, the

stark reality of their affair having finally sunk in. She simply could not go on pretending that she didn't love him; that all she cared about was fun and games. 'Look, I'll buy a morning-after pill at the airport. They always have pharmacies at airports. Then neither of us will have to worry. Now, please…just take me home.'

He stared at her for a long moment. 'All right,' he finally said, and Harriet let out a huge sigh of relief.

When they arrived at the airport, Harriet found a pharmacy and asked for the morning-after pill. But, as it turned out, the rules in Italy were different from some other parts of the world. You couldn't just buy one over the counter; you had to have a doctor's prescription to get the pill. She was told that the public health clinic in Milan would give her a prescription, but it wouldn't be open till the following morning, and there was often a several-hours wait to be seen.

Harriet decided fate was telling her something and they boarded their flight without said pill.

'But what if you *are* pregnant?' Alex asked, face grim.

'I'll cross that bridge when I come to it. But

you don't have to worry, Alex. If I am pregnant, then I'll take care of it.'

'What do you mean by that?'

'I mean I'll take care of it,' she snapped. 'Now, if you don't mind, I don't want to talk about it any more.'

CHAPTER TWENTY-FOUR

ALEX WENT TO work extra early that Monday morning, mostly because he'd been awake for hours. Sleep had been elusive during the two and a half weeks since his return from Italy, something he wasn't used to. It had been especially elusive last night, knowing that Harriet had made a doctor's appointment for first thing this morning to find out if she was pregnant. She'd refused to use one of the home testing kits you can buy over the counter—despite being a few days late—claiming they weren't always accurate and she needed to be sure. She'd also refused to do other things, like talk to him more than strictly necessary. She wouldn't even have coffee with him.

The past two weeks at work had been sheer hell.

The moment Alex let himself into the office, the cat sauntered over to him, purring as he wound himself around his ankles.

'At least you still love me,' Alex muttered.

Not that Harriet had ever loved him. But she had liked him. And desired him. Now she couldn't seem to stand the sight of him, which really wasn't fair, in Alex's humble opinion. It wasn't *his* fault that the damned condom broke.

'Come on, Romany,' he said with a weary sigh. 'Let's go get you some food.'

That done, he made himself a mug of black coffee before taking it into his office and slumping down behind his desk. As he sat there, sipping slowly, he tried to work out exactly why Harriet was so angry with him. And she was. She tried to hide her antagonism towards him, but it had been there, in her body language, right from the time they'd had the disastrous news about the morning-after pill. Harriet had even looked perversely pleased when he'd informed her that the only seats left on the first available flight home were first class. Alex had soon twigged that this was because she would have her own space and not have to sit next to him. Or talk to him. From the moment they'd arrived back, she'd cut him dead, saying it was over between them and taking a taxi home.

Every day since, Alex had tried to work out what he would do and how he would feel if she *was* pregnant.

Clearly, Harriet had no intention of keeping the baby if she was. Her savage 'I'll take care of it' had indicated exactly what she would do. Alex knew that if he'd accidentally impregnated any other girl he'd been involved with over the years, he would not have objected to this course of action.

But you didn't love any of those girls. You love Harriet, he accepted at long last. *If she is going to have your baby, you will want her to keep it.*

Shock at this astonishing realisation propelled Alex forward in his chair, some coffee sloshing onto his tie and shirt front. Swearing, he banged the mug down on his desk and stood up, reefing his clothes off before the coffee burned his skin. Fortunately, there was a brand-new shirt and tie in the bottom drawer of his desk, courtesy of his brilliant PA, who thought of every eventuality before it had even happened.

What in God's name would he do without her? Alex's heart lurched at the very real possibility that Harriet would soon exit from his life altogether. She hadn't said anything yet, but he could *feel* it. She meant to move on, and there was absolutely nothing he could do to stop her. As time ticked away, he began to hope that she *wasn't* pregnant. Maybe then things might settle back to normal.

Not a very logical thought.

The next two and a half hours were agony. He couldn't think about work. Instead, he tried filling in the time till Harriet arrived by ringing his father and then Sarah. His father didn't want to talk. He was off to his morning exercise class, his perky voice actually irritating Alex, which was perverse. Sarah couldn't talk, either. She had to drive the kids to school, then go on to work, saying she would talk to him later. He contemplated calling Jeremy and confiding the situation to him. But it would be the middle of the night in London and no doubt Jeremy would not be alone.

In the end, Alex wandered downstairs into the café where he'd taken Harriet that fateful day not all that long ago. After ordering a bagel and another coffee, he sat down at the same table and stared through the window at the passing parade whilst his inner tension escalated to a level he'd never experienced before. By the time a pale-faced Harriet showed up for work shortly before eleven, Alex's temples were pounding and his shoulder blades ached.

At least she didn't keep him waiting. She came straight into his office, stood in front of his desk and said bluntly, 'I'm not pregnant. So you can breathe easier now.'

He actually did let out a huge breath, having found that his heartbeat had been temporarily suspended. He could not help but notice that she noticed, a small, rueful smile on her lips.

'The doctor said I'm late because I'm stressed,' she went on before he could say a single word. 'Which leads me to my next announcement. I'm resigning. Right now. I can't work for you any more, Alex. I'm sorry to leave you in the lurch like this, but you can get a temp till you can fill my position permanently. There are plenty of good agencies who specialise in excellent temps. I seem to recall you were working with a temp before you found me, so you'll know what to do. I'd take Romany with me, but animals still aren't allowed in my building. Besides, he'd miss this place now. It's his home. I'll ask Audrey to keep an extra eye on him on my way out.

'It's been a pleasure working for you, Alex,' she finished up while he just sat there, pole-axed. 'Up till recently, that is. Still, what happened was as much my fault as yours. You didn't force me to sleep with you, or do any of the other things we did together. As for a reference, I'm sure that when asked you will give me a good one. You might be a selfish man, but you're not a vindictive one. Goodbye, Alex. No, please don't say anything. I've made up my mind and you won't change it.'

So saying, she whirled and was gone, Alex staring at the empty doorway without moving a muscle till Audrey stormed in a couple of minutes later, looking outraged.

'Harriet's just left,' she informed him unnecessarily. 'She told me she'd quit, but she wouldn't tell me why. As if I can't guess!'

Alex suppressed a sigh as he snapped forward on his chair and adopted his firm 'boss face'. 'Why Harriet resigned is none of your business, Audrey. Please go back to Reception.'

'I always thought you were heartless where

women were concerned,' she spat at him. 'I just didn't realise how heartless. That girl's fallen in love with you. That's why she's quit. Blind Freddie could see how unhappy she's been these last couple of weeks. It's you! You seduced her that Friday you took her away with you, didn't you?'

'I did not seduce Harriet and she's not in love with me,' he stated, trying not to sound as shaken as he felt. 'So please don't go saying any of that to the others.'

'I wouldn't be bothered. But, just so you know in advance, I'll be looking around for another job. Even if you didn't do anything wrong with her, I don't want to work for a man who'd let a fantastic girl like Harriet just walk out without fighting to keep her. Don't you care how upset she is?'

'Of course I care. But she can be very stubborn.'

'But if she's not in love with you, then why did she leave?'

'I don't know, Audrey. Maybe it has something to do with her break-up with Dwayne. Maybe she just needs a change.'

'But she *loved* working for you.'

Alex was as close to weeping as he'd been in

decades. 'Look, I'll give her a call later and see if I can change her mind.' Even as he said the placating words, he knew he wouldn't do any such thing. It was over.

'Go back to work, Audrey,' he said.

After she left, Alex sat there for ages, thinking about everything Audrey had said.

You seduced her. She's in love with you. If she's not in love with you, then why did she leave?

Could he be wrong in assuming she *didn't* love him? If she did love him, it would explain a lot, especially if she thought he didn't love her.

And why *wouldn't* she think that, when he'd gone to such great lengths to make her understand that he didn't do love and marriage; that any relationship they had was strictly sexual?

God, but he was an idiot!

Jumping up, he pulled on his jacket, grabbed his keys and headed out, telling Audrey as he passed Reception that he was off to get Harriet back.

'Just as well,' she threw after him.

Ten minutes later, Alex was only a block from the office, stuck in traffic.

'Damn!' he swore. He thought about ringing Harriet but decided that wouldn't be good enough. He had to do this face-to-face. There was no option but to wait.

CHAPTER TWENTY-FIVE

HARRIET WAS CURLED up on her sofa, no longer crying but feeling terrible, when there was a knock on her flat door. It was a rather timid knock, so she knew it wasn't Alex come to demand she return to work. Not that he would. Alex wouldn't run after any woman.

Probably a neighbour, needing something.

It was Betty from next door, wanting to borrow an onion. She was a dear old love who found it hard enough to get up and down the stairs, let alone walk to the corner shop just to buy an onion. Harriet was happy to give her one.

'Thanks, pet,' she said. 'I saw you come home earlier. Not feeling well? You do look a little peaky.'

'I had a bad headache,' Harriet invented. 'But it's gone now. In fact, I was just about to go out for a walk along the beach.'

'Wish I could come with you, pet, but these

old legs of mine won't cooperate. Thanks for the onion.'

After Betty left, Harriet forced herself to put on leggings, trainers and a light sweater, then set off for a power walk to the beach. Exercise always did her good, as did the sight of the sea. There was something calming about watching the waves roll into shore. Something...spiritual.

The first sight of the blue ocean lifted her spirits. *You will survive this, Harriet*, she told herself. *And, just think, soon you'll have a baby to love.* How wonderful was that?

By the time Alex reached Harriet's address he was not a happy man, his frustration increasing when he couldn't find a parking spot in her street for love nor money. In the end, he parked in someone's driveway, knocked on their door and gave the startled woman a hundred dollars to let his SUV stay there for a couple of hours. Alex figured he might need a couple of hours to convince Harriet that he really, truly loved her. Lord knew what he was going to do if she didn't love him back and didn't give a damn.

It wasn't like Alex to entertain negative thinking, but it wasn't every day that he fell in love. He understood now why he'd been afraid of it. Because he had known, subconsciously, that when and if he fell in love it would be very deeply. Not to have his love returned would shatter him.

His tension increased as he hurried up the stairs of Harriet's block of flats, his heart pounding along with his feet. When he knocked loudly on her door, the sound echoed through the whole building. When she didn't answer, he knocked again. And again. And again.

A door opened along the way and an elderly lady peeped out. 'If you're looking for Harriet, she's gone for a walk along the beach.'

'Right. Thanks.'

Alex took off in the direction of nearby Bondi Beach, his long legs bringing him there in less than a minute. Thankfully, the beach wasn't all that crowded. He searched along the wide stretch of sand but didn't see her. And then she came into view, walking briskly along the promenade towards where he was standing in front of the Pavilion. She stopped as soon as she saw him, her body language not good. Her chin came up, her hands curling into fists by her sides. He couldn't see the expression in her eyes, as she was wearing sunglasses. But he got the impression of barely controlled anger and heaps of exasperation.

In the end, she covered the few metres which separated them, her hands finding her hips as she planted herself right in front of him.

'What are you doing here?' she bit out.

'I went to your flat, but you weren't there. Your neighbour told me where to find you.'

'That's not what I asked you. Look, you're wasting your time, Alex. I'm not coming back to work for you and that's that!'

'I haven't come to talk to you about work,' he returned in what he hoped was a calm voice. *Someone* had to be calm. Still, he took the level of her ongoing anger as a positive sign. She really didn't have that much reason to be angry with him. Not unless her emotions were involved.

'Neither am I going to keep sleeping with you!' she said in a voice loud enough to have passers-by stare over at them.

'Could we possibly have this discussion in private, Harry? I don't appreciate your telling the world about our personal business.'

At least she had the good grace to blush.

'Come on,' he said, taking her elbow and leading her away from several curious onlookers. 'We'll go back to your place and have things out there.'

'There are no things to have out,' she muttered.

'I beg to differ. We have lots of things to have out, mostly concerning your misconception about my feelings for you.'

Her laugh was wry and bitter. 'I was *never* in any doubt over your feelings for me, Alex.'

'You could be wrong, you know.'

Harriet knew she wasn't wrong. The only reason Alex had come after her was because he didn't like being left in the lurch, either in his office or in his bed.

'If you think you can seduce me again, then you have another think coming.'

'I never seduced you in the first place, Harry. You came to my bed willingly.'

'You know what I mean. You engineered our being alone together so it would be harder for me to resist you.'

'I plead guilty to that one.'

Wrenching her arm out of his hold, she hurried

ahead of him, not saying another word till she was standing by her front door fumbling with her keys.

'You can come in,' she threw over her shoulder at him. 'But not for long. It won't take long anyway, because there's nothing you can possibly say to make me change my mind on this. We're over, Alex. As hard as it might be for a man of your ego, I suggest you learn to take no for an answer.'

'Hell, but you don't make things easy on a man, do you?' he ground out as he strode after her into her living room. 'I almost pity poor old Dwayne.'

'I suggest you leave Dwayne out of this,' she snapped, banging the door after him and tossing her sunglasses onto the hall table. 'Now, just get on with what you have to say.'

'Okay, I will. The thing is, Harriet, that I love you. Sorry if that's not the most romantic of declarations, but it's hard to be romantic when you're this angry.'

Harriet would wonder afterwards if she looked as shocked as she felt. All she could remember in hindsight was that her heart stopped beating and her body seemed to freeze on the spot. Nothing worked. Not her brain, her tongue or anything.

He started pacing, throwing snatches of words at her as he circumnavigated the room with long, angry strides.

'I know I said I didn't do love… And I don't… or I didn't… Till you came along. You changed everything… Loving you changed everything…'

He finally ground to a halt in front of her again, his handsome face all flushed and frustrated.

'I love you, Harriet. And I want to marry you. I even want to have babies with you, which believe me is such an astonishing concept that it took me a while to get my head around it. But once I did, I saw that it could be wonderful. You'd make a marvellous mother. When you told me this morning that you weren't pregnant, I actually felt disappointed. But I could hardly tell you that because at the time I thought you didn't love me back. But then Audrey stormed in and told me that you probably did. So then I got to thinking that maybe you did love me, that that was the reason for your anger. But now that I'm here, I'm not so sure.'

He took abrupt hold of her shoulders and dragged her close. 'Tell me that I'm not wrong, Harry,' he demanded in a passionate voice which fairly vibrated through the air. 'Tell me that you love me, because if you don't, I don't know what I'll do.'

Harriet's eyes swam with the impact of his declaration. He loved her. Alex loved her. He even wanted to marry her and have babies with her. Oh, God…

'Please don't cry,' he said, then gathered her to him. 'Just tell me that you love me.'

'I love you,' she choked out against his throat. 'Oh, Alex…'

His heart almost burst with happiness and relief. She loved him. She really loved him.

'And you'll marry me, even if I don't tick your check-boxes for a husband?'

'You tick the most important ones. But, Alex…'

His heart tightened at the sudden wariness in her voice. Holding her at arm's length, he looked deep into her still-teary eyes. 'What is it? What's wrong?'

'Nothing. I hope… It's just that I…I never

imagined that you loved me. You were always so adamant that our relationship was about nothing but fun and sex. I honestly believed that if I was pregnant you'd try to talk me into having a termination. So I lied to you this morning. I lied and I…I'm sorry…'

His shock was evident. But it was quickly followed by delight. 'So you *are* pregnant?'

She nodded, still looking slightly guilty. 'I thought I was doing the right thing at the time.'

'I can understand that. So you were planning on raising our child all alone, were you?'

'I…I might have told you about it when it was too late for a termination.'

'I sincerely hope so. Still, you're going to *have* to marry me now,' he said, smiling.

'If you insist.'

'I insist.'

He kissed her then, the kissing leading to more than kissing. Lots more. Finally, they moved into her bedroom. Afterwards, Harriet snuggled into Alex's arms, happier than she'd ever been in her life.

'I can't believe that you love me,' she murmured.

'Fishing for compliments, Harry?' he said softly and kissed the top of her head.

'Not really. But feel free to give them, if you like.'

He laughed. 'In that case, be assured that I love everything about you, including your obsessive sense of independence.'

'I'm not that bad. Surely?'

'You don't think it obsessively independent to not tell the father of your child that you're pregnant?'

'I would have told you. In the end.'

'I hope so. So when are we getting married?'

'Not too soon. I don't want a rushed wedding, Alex. How about we have the wedding in that little chapel you're building up at the golf resort?' she suggested, thinking it would be romantic to marry near where they'd first got together.

'But that won't be finished for months!' he protested.

'Does it matter?'

'Would you live with me in the meantime?'

'Of course. But I won't be selling this flat. It can be the beginning of my property portfolio.'

'Done!' he said. 'What about work? Will you come back to work for me?'

'I don't see why not.'

'Thank God for that. If you don't, I would never be able to show my face around there ever again. Audrey called me heartless. She even threatened to get another job. The only one who loves me there is Romany.'

'Don't be silly. Everyone there loves you. You're a great boss.'

'I don't care about everyone else. Just about you.'

'Oh, Alex…' The tears came hard and fast then, tears of happiness and relief, all the emotion and tension Harriet had been bottling up over the past month finally set free.

Alex drew her close, his heart squeezing tight at the thought that he might have lost her today. Lost her *and* his child. It had been a close call. Too close for comfort. Never again, he vowed, would he let her doubt his love for her. Never, ever again. And, as he held her even closer, he felt sure that his mother would be pleased that he'd finally found true love with a wonderful girl like Harriet. Being a philanthropist was all very well, but being a good husband and father was just as important.

'By the way,' he whispered into her hair. 'After the wedding, I'm taking you to Venice for our honeymoon.'

* * * * *

In case you missed it, book one in the
RICH, RUTHLESS AND RENOWNED *trilogy,*
THE ITALIAN'S RUTHLESS SEDUCTION,
is available now!
And look out for book three, Jeremy's story,
coming soon!

Uncover the wealthy Di Sione family's sensational
secrets in the brand-new eight-book series
THE BILLIONAIRE'S LEGACY,
beginning with
DI SIONE'S INNOCENT CONQUEST
by Carol Marinelli
Also available this month

MILLS & BOON®
Large Print – November 2016

Di Sione's Innocent Conquest
Carol Marinelli

A Virgin for Vasquez
Cathy Williams

The Billionaire's Ruthless Affair
Miranda Lee

Master of Her Innocence
Chantelle Shaw

Moretti's Marriage Command
Kate Hewitt

The Flaw in Raffaele's Revenge
Annie West

Bought by Her Italian Boss
Dani Collins

Wedded for His Royal Duty
Susan Meier

His Cinderella Heiress
Marion Lennox

The Bridesmaid's Baby Bump
Kandy Shepherd

Bound by the Unborn Baby
Bella Bucannon

MILLS & BOON®
Large Print – December 2016

The Di Sione Secret Baby
Maya Blake

Carides's Forgotten Wife
Maisey Yates

The Playboy's Ruthless Pursuit
Miranda Lee

His Mistress for a Week
Melanie Milburne

Crowned for the Prince's Heir
Sharon Kendrick

In the Sheikh's Service
Susan Stephens

Marrying Her Royal Enemy
Jennifer Hayward

An Unlikely Bride for the Billionaire
Michelle Douglas

Falling for the Secret Millionaire
Kate Hardy

The Forbidden Prince
Alison Roberts

The Best Man's Guarded Heart
Katrina Cudmore